SAURIAN SAFARI

BY BRIAN GATTO

SEVEREDPRESS

SAURIAN SAFARI

WWW.SEVEREDPRESS.COM

ISBN: 978-1-923165-57-1

CHAPTER ONE

It had passed.

The torrential storm had passed like a gust of wind carrying a warm breeze across the Atlantic Ocean. It had been quick, akin to the afternoon showers in central Africa. The jungle was now damp. Its trees saturated, the ground mushy to the touch. There had not been a storm like it in a few seasons.

Before the storm, the winds had been harsh. It carried the ominous clouds that had arrested the skies and locked them into a temporary grey. The powerful gales knocked down thick brush and even some of the taller trees in the terrain. It had remained off the common pathways, at least common to the locals who inhabited the region. It brewed deep within. No one had ever traveled through these thicks. No machete was durable enough, no machine could crunch through.

They feared that part of the jungle. Knowing of the hungry eyes that dwelled in the darkness and the tales that had clung to the wood line of that hideous section of untapped world. It was not uninhabited. Other stories of feral tribes existing in that disturbingly grim part of the Congo sent shivers down the spines of the children in the neighboring villages. It made their mothers feel faint.

Uncommon but not unheard of, outsiders would come. They attempted to investigate the massive number of disturbances and disappearances the remote place had caused. One such man, a Congolese National Policeman by the name of Rocco Camu, had tried to trek into the forbidden landscape with a handful of hunting scouts to track down a supposed predator stalking a nearby village. They had not succeeded. Two of the party, young and adventurous, took a few steps into a sliver of clearing and were immediately lost. Only one of them was found. The other had vanished as did their entry point.

What remained of the party had gone back to the town to report their failure. There were no further attempts. That is until now.

The date, January 19th, 2008. It was during the dry season they came. A trio of explorers entered the town of Kindu.

One of them, Sarah Denning, carried a crossbow and a chip on her shoulder. She seemed to have an attitude towards the world. She, along with the others, entered a small shack. The thatched roofs gave little protection from the beating sun. It seeped through relentlessly. One ray of light fell upon a desk made of a marble countertop and aged oak wood. There were bamboo sticks along the front to give it a more appropriate appearance.

Sarah lay her crossbow down and looked at the man sitting behind the desk. "We're here to see someone. His name is Rocco."

"Ah, yes, Rocco." The male spoke in broken English. "He's sitting over at the bar, over there."

He pointed across the room to a minibar with an emphasis on mini. It had two chairs and an even smaller counter than the service desk. Sarah and her two companions made their way over. Before they reached him, he looked up. "You come recommended from the Conners."

"Yes, we do," the man to Sarah's left, a wiry, all business individual with the scientist look down pat, stated.

"That was not a question." Rocco got up from his seat. "I'm at your service."

He gave a mock salute and began towards the exit. There was no door to the shack, so he just stepped outside. Sarah chased after him.

"We need to go over where we're going!" she exclaimed.

"I have a pretty good idea. It's not rocket science. You want what I saw."

"And what was it you saw?" the scientist asked.

"Look, Mr…"

"Ward. Allister Ward."

"Well, okay, Mr. Ward. Please don't jerk me around. I know why you're all here." Rocco took a step forward towards the timid man. "I just want this trip to go as smoothly as possible. No hiccups."

"Rest assured, we've worked out in the field before," the other man said. "Name's Peter Denning. I'm the brother of ol' hot head Sarah here."

Rocco looked at both of them. "You don't look like siblings."

"Six years apart makes a big difference I guess." Peter gave a beaming smile.

He paused.

"You seem apprehensive."

"I don't want any heroes either." He then marched towards a jeep.

The bright red vehicle was covered in grime and had rust on the doors and fenders.

"Nice ride," Alister scoffed.

"It's the best you're going to get in a hundred-mile radius."

They all piled in. Alister sat in the front passenger side while the siblings took up the back seat. Rocco started the engine, and a loud blast could be heard. It coughed up black smoke but suddenly kicked on and roared to life.

Alister rolled his eyes. Rocco saw but paid him no mind. He knew his kind. The sensitive type that liked to complain a lot about things that weren't a real issue. A true beta male. Rocco suppressed a smirk and drove down the beaten path.

Only a few minutes in and Alister wanted to throw up. The terrain was rough, but the jeep's shocks seemed to have little effect in toning down the bumpy ride they were all enduring. He turned to see Sarah and Peter. They appeared to be right at home. Sarah held onto the bar above her. She had no excess skin. She was attractive with pursed red lips and straight, thin brown hair that was tied back into a ponytail. Her skin had a slight tan to it from the aggressive sunlight absorption. It rather added to her beauty. Peter noticed Alister staring. The scientist turned back.

"So, what's a group like you interested in a few eggs for?" Rocco asked.

"Don't be coy," Sarah smirked.

"Whatever do you mean, senorita?" Rocco looked in the rearview mirror and smiled.

"You know as well as we do that those eggs are not normal."

"From the pictures you sent us, they appear to belong to a reptile of the unknown," Alister added.

"You guys sure came a long way from..." He paused. "Where did you say you were coming from again?" Rocco inquired.

"We didn't," Peter stated.

"Well, wherever it is, I'm sure these eggs don't belong there," Rocco continued. "The Congo may be a dangerous place. However, if reptiles such as these managed to survive, then who knows what else is out there."

"Did you see anything else?" Sarah asked.

"Only demons." He grinned.

The four sat in silence as the jeep bounced down the quickly disappearing path.

"We must walk from here." Rocco stopped the jeep.

The clearing up ahead was narrowing. It was becoming harder to see through the thick foliage around them. It was green everywhere.

"Welcome to the green hell."

He hopped out. "Red is the perfect color to spot if we get lost. This jeep could be spotted fifty feet away in the jungle."

"What if it's too thick to see fifty feet?" Sarah asked.

Rocco held up his keys and pressed a button. The alarm blared through the jungle.

"Nice." She smiled.

"How far to the eggs?" Peter wondered.

"Maybe about three miles northwest."

"Then let's get a move on. The sooner we arrive the better." Alister slung his backpack over his shoulders.

"Yes sir." Rocco gave another mock salute.

As everyone geared up, Sarah turned to Rocco. "I wonder why they're so close to civilization?"

"We push into the jungle, she pushes back," Rocco explained.

Sarah nodded.

The air was thick and humidity high. Regardless of weather conditions, Sarah knew how important this mission was. It was also clear to her how wrong the outcome might be. They were toying with Mother Nature.

Pressing onward, Rocco smacked a nearby tree with a red, powdery substance. Marking their progress every few hundred feet, he seemed to relish in covering the thick bamboo sticks and whoppingly tall African teaks. The more Alister noticed, the harder Rocco hit the trees.

Sarah barely paid any mind, instead focusing on the canopies above her. It was a clear day so far. The sun punched through the gaps in the leaf barriers causing rays of light to shine down on them. She took it as a sign of good luck. She made her way over to Peter who seemed less than enthusiastic.

"What's on your mind, little bro?"

Peter sighed. "I don't have a problem with what we're doing. I think it's a cool idea. I mean, reptiles in zoos are overrated. Why not something new yet familiar. I just don't think we're going to find anything here."

"Why do you say that?"

"Because it's not far from anywhere really. The nest he claimed to find is only a few miles in. Why would there be a clutch of eggs of this variety so close?"

"We pushed them closer," Sarah answered.

"Don't give me that Mother Nature crap. As far as I'm concerned, this animal is just cocky."

"You seriously don't think land development and human intrusion has anything to do with it?"

"As far as I'm concerned, sis, if Mother Nature had a problem with us, she'd shake us off this planet like a bad case of fleas."

Sarah chuckled. "Nice George Carlin reference."

"Thanks." He smiled.

"Let's get a move on, guys!" Alister whined from up ahead.

Rocco looked over his shoulder at Sarah. He seemed to be wondering if she was alright. Peter snorted with laughter. "Looks like you've got a secret admirer," he whispered.

Sarah did not say a word. Instead, she marched up the slowly increasing incline towards the others. Peter shrugged, shifting his rifle strap further up his shoulder.

A roaring wall of sound could be heard up ahead. Rocco guided the team towards it. The noise increased the closer they got to the point where Sarah almost wanted to cover her ears. Alister began to get his camera ready. Whatever was beyond the overgrowth of shrubbery was amazing. There was no doubt in his mind as to what it was.

The water gushed forth down a rapid and cascaded over the ledge. Past it there was a twenty foot drop off where a pool of the lukewarm liquid continued to grow. It was a dead end for the water but a pool for any passerby.

"It's beautiful!" Sarah exclaimed.

Rocco nodded. "Angel Cove is what I like to call it."

"Why's that?" Peter asked.

"Well, it's where the beautiful women of the village like to swim." He smirked.

"Women come all the way out here to swim?" Sarah asked.

"Oh yes. It may be dangerous, but the reward is magical, so I've heard."

Sarah smiled at him.

"This is nice and all, but we need to keep moving," Alister ordered.

"Why's that?" Rocco inquired.

"*Why's that?* We need to get to the nest!" Alister shouted.

"This is the nest, Mr. Ward."

"What are you talking about?" Alister was fuming now.

"Calm down, Alister," Peter raised his hands and spoke in a soothing voice. "We're all a little tired."

The professor ignored him. "Just admit it. You don't have anything to show. There are no God damned eggs! This whole thing was a waste of our time."

"You're wasting valuable time." Rocco smirked.

Taking a few steps forward, it appeared Alister was ready to strike the local guide.

"Wait! Stop!" Sarah shouted.

"Why should I?" He continued his advances.

"No! Look out!" It was Peter this time.

Something deep down compelled Alister to stop in his tracks. Whether it be divine intervention or a gut feeling. Either way, once he did, the tip of his boot touched something. It caused a small vibration that ran through his foot. Alister did a double take as he looked down. There, situated at his feet, was an egg. Not just any egg. An enormous egg. It was oval shaped and covered in moss and grime. Thankfully there was no apparent damage to the surrounding shell. He did not want to hurt whatever was inside of it. He bent down and scooped up the egg.

"Be careful, Professor." Sarah's face lit up with shock. She had not expected the man to be so careless. Especially someone so dedicated in their field.

"Are you kidding? I wouldn't harm this creature if my life depended on it!"

"What is it?" Peter asked.

"We won't know until we can get it under a fluorescence microscope back at the lab."

"A what?" Rocco inquired.

"An X-ray machine, my good man."

"Sure seems like you're acting real friendly since I showed you where the egg was."

"But of course. Why wouldn't I be?"

"You were about to strike me there a second ago."

Alister looked down from the egg at his feet. "Oh, yes. That."

"I thought scientists were supposed to be frail," Rocco laughed.

"We've been known to be stubborn," Alister chuckled.

"Short-tempered is more like it," Sarah joined in the amusement of the situation.

Peter seemed to be the only one not content with sharing their awkward humor. In fact, he was nervous, on edge. "Hey, Doc. If this is a nest, where are the other eggs?"

The others looked around. Rocco pointed past Sarah. "I believe there were some in that patch of grass on the other side of the lagoon."

"Let's go check it out." Alister seemed almost giddy. The prospect of fame and fortune never ceased to change a man as far as Rocco was concerned. In the Democratic Republic of the Congo, greed was all too common. Law enforcement could be acquired at a cheap price. They were paid for and then bought as far as Rocco was concerned.

"I'm going to the top of the waterfall to get a better vantage point," Sarah declared.

She did not wait for a response. Instead, she began to make her way around the bend and then back up towards them. Peter watched his athletic sister as she made a quick pathway with her machete and effortlessly positioned herself at the peak.

"I'll go up there too. I know not to mess with Mother Nature." He tipped his Boonie hat and followed the carved-out section of jungle she had obliterated with her blade.

Alister was already skimming through the tall blades of aquatic plants like Bolbitis and barnyard grass such as Enchinochloa. Lily pads drifted further and further away the deeper he dug. Peter walked around him and leaned against a mahogany tree.

"Aren't you going to help me?" Alister wondered.

"We're just your protection."

"I'll make sure you get a bonus."

"Where have I heard that one before?" Peter scoffed.

Continuing his search, the professor was completely oblivious to the fact that Sarah and Rocco were high above him. She had her crossbow pointed right past him while Rocco stood watch.

"Seems like a nice view," he said with a smile.

Sarah did not pull her eye away from the lagoon. "Looks can be deceiving."

"I take it I did something wrong?"

"Well. No," she stated. "I just think the amount we're paying you wouldn't seem reasonable for what you brought us to."

"Ah, I see. Monetary confusion."

"More like momentary confusion. I think I had you all wrong."

"Oh?" Rocco wondered.

"You're not here to bring the beast to us. You're here to bring us to the beast." She slowly stood up and spun around pointing her weapon at their guide.

Rocco took on a look of shock. He was not appalled though. "I can understand your hostility."

"Can you?" Sarah asked.

In response, he reached for his blade. "I'll disarm myself."

"Don't bother." Peter came up behind him and unsheathed his Bowie knife.

"What do you think you'll accomplish by taking these eggs out of here?" Rocco's face turned beet red.

"More than you'll ever understand," Sarah said.

"You are the ones who don't understand! My kid brother was part of the first search party that disappeared in this part of the jungle! He took one step in and entered a green hell!"

"Sounds like he got lost." Peter looked to his sister and then back to Rocco.

Rocco slowly turned around to face him. "He did not get lost. He was eaten. Just like his best friend Juan and just like you'll all be."

"What is it to you? A God?" Sarah asked.

"No. A monster." Rocco spat in Peter's face and then whirled around and knocked Sarah's hands upward.

She did not lose her grip on the crossbow but did begin to stumble around as she lost her footing. By the time Peter recovered, Rocco was upon him. He did not beat him but rather pinned him down.

"You won't need an X-ray to tell you what are in the eggs. You'll find out soon enough!" Rocco laughed.

"Look out!" Alister called from below.

A massive pair of claws clamped around Rocco's shoulders. He was then hoisted off the ground and into the air just as Sarah lost her balance and fell over the side of the waterfall.

Without dropping the egg he had carefully tucked under his armpit, Alister waded out into the lagoon. His raincoat began to poof out behind his shoulders acting as a makeshift flotation device.

Peter could only watch as Rocco was carried away screaming. He cried and pleaded for help all the way until the freakish bird-like reptile lowered its head and clamped down on his. It then made a couple of twisting motions and yanked upward, decapitating him. The severed head fell from its beak and landed in the lagoon right between Alister and Sarah.

She was reaching down for her crossbow but could not find it.

"Leave it!" Alister shouted.

Suddenly, she dipped below the water. Diving down, she looked around. Thankfully, the water was clearer than she presumed it would be. Still, there was no sign of her bow.

Alister looked up and saw that Peter was looking ahead. He presumed he was seeing several more of the flying reptiles crawling on their wings towards him. As they scurried, he had to make a split-second decision. He stood up and peered over the waterfall.

"You can do it!" Alister called up to him.

Mmmrawww.

A screeching caw sound could be heard. Peter looked over his shoulder and saw the bloody clawed creature swooping down to make another attack.

"You ain't taking me under your wing," Peter laughed.

By the time he leapt, it was too late. One of the grounded Pteranodons lunged for him. It narrowly missed but swung its head, knocking into Peter's left side.

It was about to flap its wings, no doubt to scoop him up and carry him away when a sharp whistle sound split through the air and resulted in an arrow penetrating its right eye. It fell to the ground and flailed about.

In freefall, Peter prepared himself for the eventual impact of body to water. He covered his nose and began to stretch out in a diving formation.

Unbeknownst to him was how close the other Pteranodon was. It outstretched its claws. They were within a hair of gripping onto his shoulders when something hard landed on its back. Peter landed in the water none the wiser. He dove and managed to glide along the bottom for about ten feet. When he resurfaced, he saw the two Pteranodons locked in combat. One had an arrow in its eye while its beak was embedded in the other's stomach.

Alister and Sarah fished him out of the water and began to tear through the jungle. Without a guide they were lost. It was only his handy red markings that led the way. They were losing light fast though.

The trek took its toll on all of them. Sarah and Peter shared surprise that Alister had not complained once. The dark jungle held a foreboding sense of dread as the noises came and went. Predators were stalking them, that much was clear. Soon, they found another marking.

Peter fished something out of his pocket. "Little souvenir from our departed guide."

He clicked a button, and an alarm went off. It rang all too familiar.

"The home stretch, you guys!" Sarah cheered.

Mmmrawww

The three spun in unison and saw a flock of Pteranodons descending upon their location.

"Yeah, well. We'd better hurry!" Alister's voice quivered.

The three marched through the jungle. Peter ran ahead of them as they got closer to the jeep. He hopped in and started the ignition. The headlights turned on and blazed through the blackness.

What Peter saw froze him momentarily in his place.

They were hideous. Dark green with some black stripes on their sides, bright red gums and yellow angular teeth, the predators sneered at him as if they were caught red handed.

He quickly raised himself from the driver's seat and stood up. He unslung his rifle and rested his elbow on the window frame bar. He took a few shots and only one found their target. Continuing the fire, he managed to hit two more of the devilish creatures.

"What the hell are you shooting at?" Alister cried out. "It certainly is not the birds!"

He and Sarah did not bother looking back until they climbed in.

"My God," Alister said.

"What are they, Doc?" Peter asked.

"You, my friend, are either very lucky, a good shot, or both."

"Why's that?"

"It seems we have more saurian specimens to collect out here after all."

"Uh, what?" Sarah asked, dumbfounded.

"Not only is there a surviving flock of Pteranodons out here that can successfully breed and produce young, but there seems to be one other species out here as well."

"C'mon, out with it, Doc!" Peter said impatiently.

"Are they raptors?" Sarah asked.

"No, worse." He pulled off his glasses and quickly cleaned them off before placing them back over his eyes. "Utahraptor."

CHAPTER TWO

The day had come.

For Francis Conners, it was one of great accomplishment. For the dinosaurs, it was a migration nightmare. They had forcefully been hauled out of their domain, loaded into cargo ships, and shipped across the Atlantic Ocean. Little did the entrepreneur mind the sea. The massive waves that smashed into the vessel with the force of a charging rhino did little to cause a stir amongst his drink. There was not the faintest ripple. He sat back in his lounge chair as his wife lay on the deck on a pink and white striped towel sunning herself.

Megan Conners was a beautiful forty-eight years old woman. Barely any sign of age. She had the occasional bags under her eyes from her long hours spent in the lab with Alister Ward, going over different locations and theories as to where the creatures would reside. Other than that, she was gorgeous. Her dirty blonde hair had a nice curl to it as it lay over her shoulder in a bunchie ponytail.

She pushed herself up on her hands and arched her back. Her yellow bikini shone across the Atlantic as her cleavage glistened in the harsh sunlight. "I can't believe we've come this far."

"We sure have come a long way from beakers and sample tubes," he chuckled.

"Those displays did help us even consider the Congo as a possibility."

"That and the local population disappearing more so than usual."

This was the third trip. Second the Conners had accompanied the team on. The first haul had corralled a trio of Utahraptor and a large egg that belonged to a Pteranodon. The second was their most successful. Sarah and Peter had managed to acquire an infantine Stegosaur, and two tyrannosaur adults, one of which was pregnant. On their way back to the ship they traveled through the swamp and snagged a Spinosaurus.

This trip was a little less bountiful. Below the deck was a Baryonx, two Dilophosaurus, and a Dimetrodon found in the same swamp as the Spinosaurus.

"We're going to need more herbivores to offset the carnivores," Francis stated.

"I'm sure the next trip will prove rewarding." Megan smiled at her husband.

"The locals won't like that," Francis sighed.

"After the incident with Rocco I thought they would not intervene anymore," Megan said. "I think they've taken the hint though."

"Maybe." Francis nodded.

Megan smiled at her husband and stood up. She sauntered over to the radio situated on a nearby table and clicked the play button. U2's *Stuck in a Moment You Can't Get Out Of* came on with drums blaring. She then looked over her shoulder and grinned. Her bright teeth melted his heart. Then, she began to mouth the chorus and dance over to him.

"What are you doing?" he chuckled.

Slowly she leaned over and climbed on him. Her continued lip syncing was irresistibly cute. Then they leaned towards each other to kiss.

"Ahem," a familiar voice interrupted them.

Both Megan and Francis turned to see the first mate of the cargo ship. He had the same stern look on his face he always had and that no one could decipher. He held out his burley arm and handed Francis the satellite phone. "Phone call, Mr. Conners."

"Thank you, Morris."

He groaned and made his way down the metallic steps, his boots clinking with each step.

Francis held the sat to the side of his face. "Hello?"

"Mr. Conners. I hope the timing is not inconvenient, but I have an update on that new specimen." Alister's voice came on over the phone.

"Oh?"

"I can send out a chopper to come get you and Mrs. Conners. There's been an update at the Beijing base."

"That's a near day-long trip, Mr. Ward."

"Trust me. Not only will it be worth it, but you'll want to be there in person."

Francis thought about it. A trip to China was not on his schedule. He was accustomed to long flights. His wife on the other hand. "How long until you can get the bird out here?"

"Give us a few hours. She's just refueling."

"I want first class for me and Megan."

"It'll cost a pretty penny," Alister said.

"You know me, Mr. Ward. There is no expense too great."

"In that case, I'll be coming with you."

"I might as well take my private plane," Francis chuckled.

"It'll be cheaper to use the airlines than spending all that money on fuel."

"I concur. In that case, I'll save you a seat."

"Much appreciated, Mr. Conners."

"Don't mention it. Oh, and by the way. What is the new specimen they've acquired this time? It better not be some old dried up husk of a caveman. Need I remind you; the park is for reptiles only."

"You're not far off but it is still within the boundaries of your dream."

Francis could practically see Alister smiling on the other end.

"Don't keep me in suspense." Francis looked down at Megan who was still sitting atop him, resting her head on his hairy chest. He was still waiting for Alister's reply. "Well?"

"Rep, hy-d." The line cut out.

"Shit." Francis hung up and closed the satellite phone. He then returned his attention to his wife. "Looks like we'll be off this rust bucket sooner than we thought."

She moaned. "Where are we going?"

He gulped. "China."

"What?"

"More specifically, Beijing."

Megan could not believe what she was hearing. "I wanted off this ship a day ago and now that I've finally got my wish you're going to bring me to the Zhoukoudian caves?"

"I've been assured it will be worth it!"

"By who? Was that Alister you were talking to? You do remember the last time we went there and all we got was a mummified corpse."

"I think it'll be different this time."Megan sighed. "You're supremely lucky I love you."

He gave her a peck on the cheek. "Thanks, babe."

Motioning off the lounge chair, he had stopped when he realized Megan was not moving.

"When do we leave?"

"In a few hours."

She smiled. "I didn't pack much."

"Neither did I."

She leaned forward for a kiss again and, this time, they held it for a full ten seconds. She then worked her hands down into his cargo shorts.

"What if someone sees?"

"Let them watch." She grinned.

"You're supremely lucky I love you." He smiled back.

***

The helicopter had arrived half an hour early. Francis and Megan were called over the intercom during their second round of lovemaking. He had almost made her orgasm. He looked up angrily at the speaker. There was a sudden urge to speak back to it. *Fuck off, we're fucking.* He held his tongue.

"They're early. We still have time." Megan pulled her husband closer.

Francis began to thrust faster. For being fifty-two, he still had enough piss vinegar to keep him going for a good couple of sessions. He would have kept going too had there not been a knock on their door. His head snapped in that direction. "We'll be right out!" There was another knock at the door.

"Busy!" Francis continued to pound into his wife.

As if the person on the other side thought the third time was the charm, he banged even harder.

"That's it!" Francis pulled out and climbed off the bed.

He stormed over towards the door and swung it open embracing the cold hallway. Alister stood there. He had not expected to see his boss fully in the nude ever but, nevertheless, there he stood. Stark naked with his manhood sticking straight up.Alister struggled to find the right words to say. "I, erm. Sorry. The walls are soundproof."

"Yeah, well. It was getting a bit too cold up on the deck to do this." Francis looked over at his wife who was covering herself up with a towel. Alister found it hard to look away.

"Probably because there's a storm coming in. The winds are picking up, cooler drafts. You know the whole shebang."

"I don't need a lesson in weather. I need you to get out of here and wait for us. We'll be out in ten minutes," Francis ordered.

"Understood." Alister backed away from the door as his boss slammed it.

He then pressed his ear against the door. He heard the cot creak and Megan moaning. Alister could hardly contain himself. He had always admired Megan for her looks. She was a model turned scientist after all. Beauty and brains. She began to nearly scream, and he almost exploded in his pants. He backed away and made his way down the hall. When he rounded the corner, he ran into Morris who looked at him stoically.

"Sound proof walls?"

"Just help your captain steer this tub."

"I presume you lost connection with Francis over the phone too and it wasn't just you pretending to do so."

"You're very nosey for a first mate."

"I've sailed for Francis for twenty years. There's a difference between being nosey and being loyal."

"What's that got to do with anything?" Alister said as he pushed past the man.

"I'd be careful if I were you."

Alister looked over his shoulder as Morris turned to him. "Money brings monsters."

The scientist gave a cocky sly grin. "Monsters bring monsters."

***

The ride to Cape Town, South Africa proved more of a challenge than once thought. While the aircraft was top of the line, no helicopter in existence would provide smooth passage through a raging storm such as this. Dark looming clouds that did not seem to move, hung in the air like stationary monstrous gas.

Rain pelted the glass with dull thuds and hit the outside like small stones being thrown at a tin can.

"Are we nearing the airport yet?" Alister asked between gags.

"Hopefully another twenty minutes," the pilot, a bearded guy without his aviators, spoke into his headset.

"I don't think I can make it that long." Alister felt the vile bile pushing up from his throat again.

"Quit complaining," Megan said.

Easy for you to say. You two are all relaxed after your little session earlier. Alister looked at Francis and Megan.

Both did seem very much in tune with the storm. Nothing was bothering them.

Megan could not help but feel creeped out by his continuous staring and had to fight not to speak her mind in the tiny shuttle they occupied. She brushed a lock of blonde hair out of her face and turned her attention to the window. A wall of water that continuously fell from the sky made for limited visibility.

There was a sudden, blinding flash followed by a loud bang of thunder that could be heard over the rotors. Then it went dark again. Her eyes adjusted and the rain became visible. She continued to stare out, not sensing anything more than just a really bad storm. It was not hailing as far as she could tell. It was hard to deduce in a car let alone a thousand feet in the sky.

Then came another light show. This time, there were a couple of flashes. In them, Megan could swear she saw something. It was huge. A dark mass with what looked like a rod sticking out of where a cone-shaped head would be. It was there for only a split second before it disappeared into the black void.

"Did you see that?" Megan turned to her husband.

Francis looked across her and then past the window. He held his gaze for a few seconds. "I don't see anything."

"It's probably just your mind playing tricks on you," the pilot stated.

"It looked like a species of avian reptile but full grown," Megan described.

"We're too far from the Congo for them to have traveled. The Atlantic's a big ocean."

"No shit! It doesn't make it impossible," Megan shouted.

She rested her head on Francis' shoulder.

"We've still got a long way to go, honey. The plane should be ready by the time we arrive. Try to get some rest." Francis calmed her.

No one spoke for a while, which helped her drift off to sleep. In her dreams, she saw her daughter marrying a nice young man and grandkids running by her own feet. It was something she had wanted ever since Daisy was a teenager. She wanted more kids but realized she was getting too old and trying to live life to the fullest. Her hopes and ambitions were interrupted when the skids of the aircraft touched down on the helipad.

***

The ship was almost to port when tragedy struck.

Benson, a regular on Morris' cargo runs, was ready to get off and go home. He had received word shortly after the Conners left that his mother had been struck by a car and was hospitalized. He had stormed onto the bridge where Morris and some other crewmembers were. He pleaded to radio back in the chopper, but the storm was too fierce to do so. On top of that, no pilot would come out this way. They could not risk lives in an attempt to save lives, let alone get someone back in a family emergency. Especially if the family member in question was not dead.

Furious, Benson stepped outside and took a few puffs of his cigarette. It had smoldered down near the butt and was starting to burn his fingers. He flicked it into the sea and reached for another one. The pack was empty.

"Goddamnit." He stood there brooding. "Maybe Cortland has some."

He marched down the steps and through the door nearest the living quarters. He walked down a flight of stairs and ended up in the massive hangar. In it, there were three massive holding crates. He walked by them. One was labeled, *Baryonx*. Another, *Dimetrodon* which was the longest of the containments give the length of the animal. The last one was noticeably smaller. It was labeled *Dilophosaurus (2)*.

He did not help corral and load the animals on the boat. The fact that two dinosaurs fit in this tiny prison was amusing to him. He then looked around. "Hey, Courtland!"

There was no response.

"Are you on your break or something?"

Benson climbed the stairs leading to the recreational room. It too was empty. "Jesus, where are you when I need you?"

Oooooo.

There was a strange hooting sound that capped off the last word of his sentence. At first, he thought he had made it. He held his hand up to his mouth.

Then it came again. A strange owl-like call that sounded deep and gurgled. Benson looked down towards the containment section and slowly descended the steps. He carefully walked over towards where the two dinosaurs were being held.

"Hello?"

This time, there was no response.

"Why would they have owls in here?" He reached forward and pulled the small eye-level door across revealing nothing but blackness. *Surely if there's a dinosaur in here, two for that matter, they couldn't hurt me when I'm this far away.*

Two pairs of glowing yellow eyes suddenly materialized out of the dark.

He had hunted enough jungles at night to know an animal had night vision when their eyes lit up a certain way. At the very least, they were nocturnal hunters and would, therefore require such a vision. He also knew that, unless they were perched on a pole, these creatures were too big to be owls.

"Huh, interesting." He went to slide the viewing door shut.

Oooooo.

There was that sound again. He paid it no mind and continued to slowly close them in there. He did not want to do it too fast else he scare them. He would rather not have to explain to Morris why his cargo was acting up and banging against the walls of their containment.

Hawk coooo.

A slimy, inky black substance shot out of the dark and directly into Benson's eyes. He nearly stumbled back as he screamed but tripped over his own feet. As his cries filled the hangar, he managed to open his eyes. He could not see anything. Then came an agonizing, stinging pain under his chin. He reached up for whatever he could find. He got hold of the scaly surface skin and realized the animal had jabbed its claw up under and through his mouth. He felt it scraping across the roof of it. Blood spilled down to his feet. It felt like rain hitting his black work boots. He coughed and gurgled as the Dilophosaurus yanked its arm and claw back along with a chunk of Benson's lower jaw.

"Ten minutes for a break," Courtland scoffed as he entered the hangar.

He was fuming while making his way towards the recreational room. Something caught his eye. His peripheral vison did not steer him wrong as he looked over and saw a pool of blood right under cargo #3.

"What the hell?" he whispered to himself as he made his way down the steps.

As he got closer, he realized the viewing door was half open. He ducked down and inched towards it. He reached up and quickly slammed the sliding door shut. He then stood up and turned around to be greeted by a horrific sight.

Benson reached out for him as he gargled blood and spewed viscera. Some chunks of flesh fell from him and strands of sinew from torn muscle clung for dear life under his chin. His skin was as pale as his own but for different reasons.

Courtland stumbled back and slipped on the blood. He fell to the ground just as Benson collapsed atop him. Blood spilled onto his chest as it cascaded down under his chin. He screamed like a banshee which alerted two more men coming into the hangar. The alarm sent shivers down the crew of the cargo ship. Morris feared the worst. He had a bad feeling about this trip from the first voyage. Now, it was all too real.

CHAPTER THREE

A little local guidance.

Zhi Peng Li met the Conners and Alister at the airport early the next day. He was skeptical about their arrival, figuring they were a bunch of rich suits with no admiration for their team of field time. There was no sense of honorability in America anymore. Still, he put on his professional smile and feigned over enthusiastic excitement at the sight of them as they approached him. He held a card displaying their last name. It read *Conars*.

Alister was the only one who sighed at the misspelling. He was not fond of informality but also liked to pay attention to the little things. Often getting annoyed when things were tested incorrectly or when a China man misspelled a name on a piece of cardboard.

Both Megan and Francis paid no mind.

"You must be Mr. Li." Francis gave a firm handshake to the young man.

"Yes, Mr. Conners," Zhi Peng's accent was thick but understandable enough. "I am to bring you to the base."

"Well, don't keep us in suspense," Francis said cheerfully.

Zhi Peng did not get the expression, but he could tell by his positive attitude and tone of his voice that they were ready to go. "Right on."

Smirking at the attempt to sound like an American, Alister handed the driver his bag and climbed into the taxi in front of him. Zhi Peng looked confused as to why the middle-aged man was getting into the vehicle.

Francis took notice. "Didn't your boss tell you there was a third party coming?"

"Yes, but that is not our ride," Zhi Peng stated.

Alister looked at the taxi driver who did not seem amused. Especially not when there were already reservations for another gentleman to be picked up at the airport.
"You not Mr. Crang," he spoke in even worse English than the other cab driver.

Looking around the backseat as if trying to think of a way to make it seem he had not made a mistake, he concluded that there was no undermining the fact that he was hasty. He quickly got out just as another man, a Chinese gentleman in a nice tailored black suit and matching color tie, approached him. He pushed Alister out of the way and climbed in the spot he was just sitting in.

The taxi took off.

"So, Mr. Li. Which ride is ours?" Francis asked with a calm, inviting voice.

"This way." Zhi Peng began to make his way across the parking lot and towards the car rental station. There he picked up his keys and the four made their way around back. Alister did not like the situation one bit. He knew Francis could have sprung for better accommodations but figured he would keep that bit of opinionated fact to himself.

Soon, they were surrounded by small shacks with a less than inviting aura about them. There were people cooking meat over roaring fires and noodles being prepped in front of hungry customers. The smell was making Alister's stomach gurgle. He had not eaten since they boarded the helicopter. In fact, none of them had. His stomach roared with hunger again. This time, Megan heard it.

"We'll be at the base soon. We can eat there," she stated.

Flames shot up from a nearby stove and it made Alister jump out of his skin. Megan looked at him. "What's gotten into you?"

"Nothing," Alister said, clearly unsure of himself. "I just don't like being in closed off areas."

"I didn't know you were claustrophobic."

"I'm not. However, I don't feel safe here. Too many pick pocketers," he whispered.

Zhi Peng looked over his shoulder. "Everyone just trying to make honest living in these parts."

"I apologize," Alister said. "I didn't know you could hear me."

"To hear, one has only to listen," Zhi Peng chuckled slightly.

"Did you make that up?" Megan wondered.

"No. Was line from movie, *Gremlins*." Zhi Peng laughed heartily.

They all shared the amusement. Alister even began to realize he may not have been too far from home after all.

It was a few minutes later when they arrived at their transportation. It was an old, beat-up red jeep that had clearly been through the ringer a few times. Alister instantly frowned. "This is it?"

"It's the best vehicle around for the trip we'll have to make. She's been through hell. Those scars are evident. As is her experience." Zhi Peng smiled.

Megan and Francis climbed in the back while Alister reluctantly took the front passenger seat. With the keys in the ignition, Zhi Peng brought the jeep out of the parking lot and down the winding road. The path was pavement for a while before slowly transforming into a dirt road.

Stabbing hunger pains made Alister squirm in his seat as the divots became more frequent. Some grass clumps almost made him shed a tear as they were rolled over the tires. It was like Zhi Peng was aiming for them to be run over on his side. Alister tried to keep his temper in check.

It was another half an hour before they saw the base. It was a few miles down the road in a canyon.

"I feel like I am going to throw up," Alister said weakly.

"Don't worry. I'll make it quick." Zhi Peng grinned.

The insidious look on his face worried the hungry scientist. Before he could object, the jeep lurched forward. It felt like a nosedive on a rollercoaster. Alister's face turned a faint shade of green. He then felt around for a bag or something to puke into. He heard the mechanical drone of the window being rolled down on his side. He briefly turned to Zhi Peng who was giving him a cheeky smile. Then, he hung his head out the window and dry heaved the rest of the way.

Pushing through foliage, taking a few plants as souvenirs as they went, the jeep ended up parked right near the front entrance of the Beijing base. It was then, they heard it. A massive roar. It did not sound like the other dinosaurs. In fact, it was almost human.

"What the hell was that?" Francis asked.

Zhi Peng turned to face him and flashed his pearly whites. "Your latest exhibit."

They exited the jeep with great haste. Excited but also nervous, the Conners and Alister followed Zhi Peng closely. Megan felt they were using him as a human shield, which was partially true. Another facet was that he was their leader, and they were following him into unknown territory. This was also somewhat based in fact because she had never been to this base. Francis had. She was not sure about Alister.

A man opened the door for them. He was a familiar face amongst the world of paleontology. "Welcome to Base B."

"Mr. Woo." Francis gave him a nod.

"I trust you had an easy flight?"

"Hardly," Alister scoffed. "You have anything to eat around here?"

"There's a cafeteria down the hall. I'm sure you're all a bit hungry. Why don't we get something to eat and then head down to see your new specimens."

"There's two?" Francis' eyes widened.

"Surprise."

"Jason, this is great news. Yes. Let's get something to eat first."

Zhi Peng led them to the mess hall and let them be. The four sat at a round table. The room was bright and had paintings of ancient man and prehistoric lizards everywhere. Megan felt she was in a museum.

The food could not arrive fast enough as far as Alister was concerned. It was all he cared about at the moment.

"Care to tell me what it is that you've stumbled upon this time, Mr. Woo?"

Jason Woo was a part time excavator, and part time cave explorer. There were numerous studies he conducted over the years that had been published in books and magazines.

"We found a new cave system," he began. "In it, we dug for days and found all sorts of precious elements. Some were worthless. Some were not. We ended up breaking through a soft patch of dirt. It was piled up to make a wall. Whoever did it, was preserving what was inside, beyond the muck."

"What was behind the wall?" Megan inquired.

"The sediment ran high as we took it down. Huge puddles were formed. We were lucky not to cause a cave in," Jason reflected.

"Did anyone get hurt?" Francis asked.

"No. Thankfully."

Their food arrived. Sloppy joes with a side of fries. Alister did not care that it looked like dog food as he dug in. The taste was as bland as his personality.

"We entered the unchartered system and quickly discovered something," Jason grinned.

"What did you find?" Megan wondered excitedly.

"Yes, please don't keep us in suspense any longer," Francis said with a businessman monotone.

Jason savored their anticipation. He reached and grabbed the sloppy joe from his plate and took a nibble. He chewed and then decided it was time. "The cave was a chamber of sorts. It contained a high level of nitrogen gas. Enough to preserve an elephant. Except what was inside was no elephant. They were two humanoid creatures."

Francis frowned. "Mr. Woo, I told you. Saurian animals only."

"Yes, well, these two males are very different from your traditional cavemen."

"Oh?" Alister looked up from his meal. "Missing links perhaps?"

"Or just a different species entirely," Jason said.

"I would like to see these humanoids," Francis stated.

They left the table. Alister chowed down on his last sandwich before chasing after them to catch up. Proceeding down the hall, Megan realized it was rather cold within the facility.

"What's their habitat like?" she asked.

"They can adjust to any climate within reason," Jason said. "They seem to prefer it warm though. They don't care for feeling the chill."

"Are they cold blooded?"

Jason turned to her and gave her a look. He then nodded. Francis liked the sound of that; a cold-blooded human would have to be reptilian to some degree. He just knew it.

Approaching a doorway, they entered an observation room. It overlooked a large enclosure that was rather dim with red lamps high above on the ceiling. Inside there was enough flora and water to practically describe it as a jungle. Jason made his way over towards a radio mounted on the wall. He grabbed the receiver and spoke into it.

"Okay, Li. It's feeding time."

"Roger, boss," Zi Pheng's voice came over the speaker system.

The three guests wondered what exactly was within the containment area. At first, there was no movement whatsoever. Then a hatch opened above, and a large chunk of meat began to lower from the ceiling. Its slow progression kept them waiting with bated breath.

It soon hovered five feet above the grass floor. Zhi Peng could be seen above controlling the large slab of raw meat with a pole and rope. There was another man there holding the lower end behind him so that they could get a good grip on it.

There was still no motion being made towards the meat. The foliage remained still. It was quiet until a large, greenish hand parted some of the giant taro that was blocking its path. Then, it emerged. It was completely hairless and had a yellow stomach with brown spots that were somewhat patchy. Its head was too small for its massive body but it could still move around just fine.

The creature looked up and saw the meal prepared for it. Suddenly, its mouth opened, and a long tongue shot out of it. It touched the meat and then retracted quickly.

"It's acting like a frog," Francis noticed.

"Ugros," Jason added.

"Ugros?" Francis had to tear his eyes away from the sight before him to look at Jason.

"It's what the guys call him. He seems to like it." Jason said.

"Sounds like you're saying *you gross,*" Alister chuckled.

Jason thought about it for a moment. The scientist was not wrong. It was too late for a name change now though. *Ya can't teach an old dog new tricks.* "Perhaps. Still, the name stays. Whenever we call him by that he perks up."

"You said there were two?" Francis questioned.

"Be lucky you can't see the other one."

"Why's that?" Megan asked.

"If you think Ugros is hideous, just wait until you meet Hysyr."

"Hysyr?" Alister laughed. "Where do you people come up with these names?"

"We used to call to him with a hi sir. That's all he would respond to. We just combined the names together. Just with a 'y' in place of the 'I' letters."

"Interesting." Franics beamed with excitement.

That all faded when a massive roar practically shook the enclosure walls. Ugros was just reaching up for the meat when a massive humanoid creature, twice the size, came barreling through the jungle-like environment. With one push, Hysyr knocked Ugros down onto his rear. He then reached up and tugged hard on the meat suspended above them. It was so unexpected that Zhi Peng and his companion nearly fell forward.

"Let it go!" Jason shouted.

"We can't! It could be used as a weapon!" Zhi Peng shouted over his mouthpiece.

Jason watched as his friend struggled with the rod. Its high-tension wire line was beginning to fray as the pole itself was bending like a big catch some fisherman just landed. This would be too big for anyone to haul in by brute force. Megan let out a yelp as Zhi Peng leaned forward followed by pulling back hard. He was treating it as if he were an angler hauling in some tuna.

"We can retrieve it after, Zhi Peng!" Jason called out again. "Just let the damned thing go!"

His employee behind him was growing tired and nervous, a deadly combo. He was not sure how this would pan out. The scenario had never been accounted for before. They usually fed them and they were gentle enough. Something had gotten into Hysyr. His attitude had changed so suddenly. He let out a massive roar that chilled the fellow meat wrangler to his core. Stumbling back, the man let go of the pole.

"Shit!" Jason ran across the observation room and out the front door.

Megan and Alister could only watch as Zhi Peng single handedly held on for dear life. He was a one-man army fighting against a *King Kong*-sized frog man. A terror unlike any other with brains and muscles.

The door off to the side of the exhibit opened and Jason ran out holding a weapon of sorts in his grip. He trudged through the grass and foliage like some mad soldier heading into combat. Taking a kneeling stance, he situated himself on his right knee and aimed the tranquilizer gun at the behemoth.

Francis came to the doorway where Jason once was. He watched in abject horror as Hysyr gave one final tug which sent Zhi Peng sprawling twenty feet downward. The entrepreneur sprinted as fast as his middle-aged legs would take him. He stopped right where he figured the man would fall. He held out his arms.

A sudden realization swept over him. He had over calculated where Zhi Peng would land. He was going to hit the ground a mere five feet in front of him. He could only stand there and watch as the zoo handler spiraled from twenty feet in the air to five feet. The impact would not be survivable.

A pair of big green hands reached out off to the side. Zhi Peng landed in them. Tears covered his face as they rolled down his cheeks. He looked up and saw Ugros standing there with a grin on his face. At first, he was elated but he looked behind Ugros and saw something that made him want to weep all over again.

Hysyr was charging for them. He leapt into the air and came down with a thunderous crash. He did not land on his designated target, instead crashing onto the soft grass with three darts sticking behind his neck.

Francis opened his eyes slowly. He half expected to see the mushy carcasses of Ugros and Zhi Peng splattered all over the ground. Instead, what he saw, was perplexing. At first, it looked like the froggish man was hugging the zoo handler. Then he realized he was protecting him. Behind them both was the mighty Hysyr, snoozing the rest of his day away.

"I'm sorry, Mr. Conners. I don't know what…" Jason began to apologize.

The entrepreneur held up his hand to silence him. He then lowered it while pointing at Ugros. "I want him."

CHAPTER FOUR

The journey only grew longer.

Permits were one thing Francis could handle. It was the shady cover-ups he did not look forward to hearing about. The call came from Morris nearly fifty seconds after they landed back in Africa. The ship had arrived with the cargo fine enough. There were some agitated Dilophosaurus. The extent of what had happened aboard was kept hidden from Francis until he and Morris could have a safe place to talk.

They both knew there would be reporters snooping around, trying to catch the big scoop. It was the sheer number of them that bothered Francis. They were coming out of their news vans in droves. Morris ushered Francis out of the public eye briefly while Megan and Alister took in the questions.

"Just what in the hell is it that you want?" Francis shrugged the captain's grip off his shoulder "Over the phone you said there was some kind of emergency."

"I couldn't specify. You know how the media likes to tap wires."

Francis nodded. "Okay then. What's the issue you have me so flustered about?"

Morris took a deep breath. "One of my crewmembers, Benson, decided to get a little nosey."

"They knew what they were transporting," Francis stated.

"Yes. They knew. They did not understand though."

"What do you mean?"

The captain shook his head. "He's dead."

"What?" Francis said a little too loud.

Morris raised and lowered his hands in a calming gesture. "Keep your voice down."

"How?" Francis whispered sharply. "How did it happen?"

"The Dilophosaurus seemed to be able to mimic the hooting sound of an owl. He went to investigate because of this reason I presume. It's like you said. Everyone knew what we were transporting. It probably struck him as odd."

"This can't be happening." Francis placed his hands on his face.

"I already told his family. Said he was mauled by a jaguar we were transporting."

"For fucks sake!" Francis looked up. "Things were already a bit dangerous in Beijing. Now we have an actual fatality."

"It could always be worse," Morris stated.

"How?"

"They could have gotten loose."

Francis tried not to seem too optimistic. The idea that the trip had gone without a massacre was a relief. "What should we do about this?"

Morris did not miss a beat. "We'll be offloading Benson during the night hours. No one will be around to see the procedure."

"Procedure?" Francis inquired.

"He was a man of the sea, Mr. Conners."

A momentary shock came over Francis before he fully realized why. "You wouldn't?"

"It wouldn't be the first time." Morris patted Francis' shoulder. "It's the first time with one of your cargos though. You can rest easy with that fact."

The captain left the entrepreneur with his thoughts. Soon, Francis made his way back over to the throng of reporters. He masked the dreadful look on his face as best he could with a cheery smile. It was all a sham.

Strong wind currents suddenly blew past everyone as a massive helicopter swooped by. They all recognized it as one of the Beijing base's choppers. Soon, it found a place to land on a nearby helipad and the doors quickly opened.

Jason Woo did not wait for the rotors to slow. He instantly ducked down and ran forward. Francis met up with him first followed by Megan, Alister, and a few straggling reporters.

"What are you doing here?" Francis was more annoyed than joyful.

"Well, I figured I'd see that our specimen has made it safely to the harbor."

"I could have called you."

"Yes, well. That's not the only reason I am here," Jason continued. "I looked at the showcasing, I felt Zhi Peng was more than ready to run the facility while I took a much-needed break. Mind you, my idea of a break is to come work at the place that started it all."

"My staff is full." Francis turned to leave.

The zookeeper placed a hand gently around Francis' wrist. "They don't know him."

"I have someone who's coming to visit that I think will."

"Oh?"

"Let's just say she's equally if not more qualified."

"Interesting. Hopefully he responds well to her commands. Still, I think I should be there. At least for a second pair of eyes."

Francis nearly bit his tongue. "I need you back at the Beijing base pronto. We have so much work to do and only a few months to get it done."

"I guess I should have kept you up to date more," Jason said suddenly. "The Beijing base has been done for two weeks. All systems check out as do the safety procedures."

Now Francis was fuming. "That's a lot to not tell me."

"I gave you Ugros. Now you have to trust me."

"Who's Ugros?" a female reporter approached them.

"Get back with the others," Francis snapped at her.

"He's something that will be worth the wait. Trust us," Jason said calmly.

Surprisingly, the reporter took the hint and backed off. Francis turned to Jason. "I don't want any more damn surprises."

"Let me tag along, at least until the zoo opens," Jason pleaded.

Francis slowly nodded. "One more miscommunication and I will have you demoted."

"I understand." He held out his hand for a handshake.

In fear of looking bad with the media, he reluctantly took it. It was not as firm as he would have liked but it would have to do. A seal of approval. A seal of fate.

***

The trip back to the compound was not as arduous as it had been a month ago. Peter had overseen the path clearing process. Deforestation as Megan called it. Francis had reassured her it was not as bad as some villages where the trail goes for miles. This was only a few hundred feet.

Palm trees lined the driveway as they went. Jason felt he was on some sunny Hollywood boulevard. He had to keep reminding himself this was Africa.

Three white U-Haul trucks trailed behind their red jeep. Each carried a species of dinosaur. Behind them was a black SUV which Alister drove. Francis and Megan were relieved by the brief reprieve of not having to be around him.

Alister was in charge of making sure no one followed them. Peter had implemented a system strictly to detect vehicles of all sizes. He had acquired it years ago in Beijing from some independent tech contractor that was in need of further funding. That was the last time Peter had visited China. He had wondered how things were going at that base.

Francis wished he could have invited him and Sarah to tag along for the trip. The team to capture these creatures was growing. The siblings were his most trusted hunters. Things needed to run smoothly at the park. He had reassured them next time they could both go.

Jason watched as the jungle practically parted away as if by some supernatural force and it gave way to the park. He slumped back into his chair.

The design of the park was the same as the one in Beijing, but the presentation was completely different. Vines twined along the walls as a variety of tropical plants surrounded the buildings. Some were red, yellow, most were a lush green. The windows were not glass paned but rather barred off with thick sticks of bamboo. Some carefully placed rocks and stones surrounded the property. Many had interesting shapes. There was one that could pass for a hippo's back. One was spray painted white with black stripes like a zebra. There was a layer of dirt that patched the sidings, which were themselves a yellowish tan.

"It's a bit rustic," Jason said flatly.

"Gives it more of a fitting feel, I think." Francis beamed at the sight of his zoo. His kingdom.

To him it was an empire 65 million years in the making. "Take a walk through Saurian Safari. Experience all the creatures and exhibits we have to offer. It's like no other experience in the world."

"Save it for the tourists," Megan said without malice. Her tone was sweet and endearing.

"Yes dear," Francis sighed.

They parked in front of the visiting center while the three U-Hauls drove carefully towards the zoo portion of the park. Alister pulled up next to the jeep. He hopped out and stretched his hands outward. "It's good to be back."

***

"I can't believe you're not going to Mallorca with us," Rebecca Stone shouted with defiance.

"I'm sorry. I already promised my parents I would visit and told *you* in advance a month ago."

The radio in the dorm was blasting *New Divide* by Linkin Park as the two argued. It somehow added to the inner flames the exchange was producing. Both women stared each other down.

"I just don't get you, Daisy?" Rebecca stated.

"I don't expect you to."

"I thought we were friends."

"We are. We just have different ideas of vacations."

Rebecca crossed her arms. "What does *that* mean?"

"It means that I don't like being groped by men while I drink my worries away."

"Are you.." Rebecca scoffed. "Are you calling me a slut?"

"No. I just want what's best for you."

"I don't need you to look after me. I can handle myself."

Daisy continued to pack. Rebbeca walked over to her slowly. "I seem to remember you being quite the party animal when you got inducted into our sorority."

"Things change. I've changed."

Rebecca laughed. "I guess you don't belong anymore then."

"What are you saying?" Daisy spun around in disbelief.

"I'm saying when you get back from visiting your parents and their little zoo, there will not be a place for you here." Rebecca crossed her arms.

Daisy turned back to her bag. "I thought we were friends."

"We were. I don't need people like you holding me back."

She sniffled and then smiled to herself. Then, she spun around and made her way into her closet. She took a few dresses, a couple pairs of jeans, and a floral top and stuffed them into her bag. Daisy Conners then stormed out of the sorority and had no intentions of ever looking back.

Getting into her Volkswagen Beetle, she turned on the radio and let her playlist tune out all her worries. The song, *Carpal Tunnel of Love* by Fall Out Boy seemed to create the perfect flow with her travels down a winding road adjacent to the ocean.

Often glancing out towards the body of water, she was consumed by pleasant thoughts. She considered Rebbeca not being in her life anymore as a positive. The party animal did not take her schooling, job on the campus, or life seriously. Daisy thought back briefly on the good times but then the bad would rush over her and she'd snap back to the present.

She began to wonder what her parents were really working on. They had been so secretive as to what the park was. She knew it had to be some kind of nature preserve. She was excepting to find reptiles the size of her car stalking the enclosed areas. It must have been something big given the fact that they were only focusing on saurian species.

Hours passed and her eyes began to grow heavy. She looked at a sign that she passed. It read that the nearest motel was forty miles. There was no chance she would be able to stay awake that much longer, so she pulled off to the side of the road.

The park was only a few more hours away. Still, she needed to sleep. She manually rolled down her window just enough so that there would be a slit wide enough to let a cool night breeze inside. The sounds of crickets and other insects filled the vehicle. She felt right at home.

Her eyelids fluttered as she began to doze off. In her dreams, she saw an abnormally shaped man. It was hard to decipher just what looked wrong about him but there was an undeniable warmth he brought about. She felt his embrace and she nestled into his chest.

Then there was a roar. Her eyes shot open. It was still night but there was light. She looked around and saw the source. A pair of headlights were beaming on her. The car door shut and the sound of stones crunching underfoot was audible. Daisy saw the small frame of a woman as she approached the car.

"Are you alright?" she called out.

"Yeah. I'm fine." Daisy rubbed her eyes.

"Do you need any assistance?"

"No. I'm alright. Just tired."

"You sure picked a funny place to sleep."

"How's that?"

"Well, I don't know if you're a thrill seeker, but parking this close to the ledge…"

Daisy looked over and saw that she was indeed close. Her front left tire was half off the cliff. "Oh shit!"

"Don't panic. Just move slowly and start your bug. Back her up carefully."

Moving faster than either one of them liked, Daisy did as she was told. The car gave a slight jerk as she went forward.

"Stop!"

She screamed as she slammed her foot on the brake.

"Put it in reverse!"

I must be more tired than I thought, Daisy said to herself as she brought the car back. She then turned off the car and opened the door where she nearly vomited.

The woman ran up to her. "That was a close one."

Daisy was breathing heavily now. Panic shook her whole body.

"It's alright. You're okay. What's your name?"

"Conners." She coughed. "Daisy Conners."

The woman stood up straight. "You wouldn't happen to be related to Francis Conners, would you?"

"What?" Daisy looked at her confusedly.

"Never mind. I'm known for my bad timing." She laughed nervously.

"I'm alright. How do you know my father?"

"I don't, at least, not personally."

"Who are you?"

"My name is Catt Brooke. I'm a reporter."

"I see." Daisy slid back into her car and was about to shut the door.

"I'm not that nosey. Are you sure you're alright?"

"Never better." Daisy smiled.

She then practically slammed the door in her face. Completing her U-turn, she sped away. Catt looked on in disbelief.

"The nerve." She laughed and then made her way back to her own car.

Daisy Conners had been pestered by reporters since she was a child. Having a disdain for them was an understatement. There was something different about the one she left behind in the trail of dust. She did not seem malicious. She then thought back again. *Who would stop for a car parked near a cliff unless they thought it would make for a good story? It's dark, it's not like she could see her clearly or have known how close she was to teetering over the edge.*

There was doubt in her conclusion, but she shrugged it off. Only a few more hours to go. *Wide awake now.*

CHAPTER FIVE

New beginnings.

As it had for hundreds of millions of years, the sun beamed against the back of trees and rays of light peeked around the corners. It was a magnificent display of natural illumination. The trees were spread apart enough to act as somewhat of a shield, but the star's powerful brightness pierced through them through every crack and chip.

Daisy Conners enjoyed the sight as she drove on the eerily quiet road. This part of the area was thick with brush on either side of the road so the sun was a warm welcome. She knew she was close to the turn off to get to the ferry and took in the sight as long as she could.

When her GPS suddenly announced for her to make the right turn down the dirt path, she obliged. She put on a pair of sunglasses and prepared herself for the light show that would soon be ahead of her. Even going as far as to squint her eyes.

She cut the corner and turned down the straight pathway. There was not much time to lose. They would wait for her but for how long she was not sure.

After a few minutes, she saw the ocean open up before her. It was as blue as her eyes that were wide with amazement. The big open area stretched for miles. She pulled up to a man who was talking with another, more agitated man.

There was a sense of fear about him that Daisy did not particularly feel comfortable about. She pulled up to them and stopped. "Hello."

"Look, she's here," the man with the calmer demeanor told his uneasy friend. "Just take her out and your contract will be up."

"No good. Dis is not a safe place ta be," he said, his accent thick.

"Babo. Please. Don't make me have to take her out there."

"I am sorry, Gerald. If ya heard what I heard, ya wouldn' wan' ta go anywhere near dat place." Babo stormed off.

Gerald turned to see Daisy's concerned expression. "These islanders and their crazy superstitions."

Daisy gave a faint smile, but she was clearly still worried.

"I assure you. Your father's island is safe."

"Have you been there?"

"Only to drop cargo and people off."

"Did you hear any strange noises like your friend claimed?"

"Babo is as skittish as they come. There's no need to worry. I've delivered there at least eight times and never heard any roaring."

"Who said anything about roaring?" Daisy's eyebrow arched.

"Well, uh, Babo, at first, claimed there was roaring coming from somewhere on the island."

"Have you talked to my parents? Are they alright?"

"Just this morning. They're excited for you to come." Gerald smiled.

Daisy thought about it. "Well, if you're sure."

"I'm positive."

She smiled and drove down further. Boarding the ferry was the hardest part. She was afraid she would go over the edge. Gerald reassured her as she came to a stop. He then went over to the consol and started the boat up.

The venture out of the harbor was short lived. It was a dinky area with a few docks and only one pair of fishermen on a small boat. She smiled and waved at them. They returned the gesture, and she noticed they barely had any teeth.

Soon, they were clear of the area and were now out on the open sea. Daisy got out of her car to stretch her legs. To her surprise, Gerald did not ogle her. Instead, he kept his attention ahead.

"How far are we from the island?"

"It's about a fifteen-minute ride. Once this haze clears you can see it from the harbor."

"Interesting," she said with genuine enthusiasm.

"It gets old after a while."

"What do you mean?"

"Babo is not the only one with wild stories about the place. I swear, they gossip too much. They're like kids spreading a curse for fun."

"Is it a joke to them?"

Gerald sighed. "No. Unfortunately. Otherwise, I'd probably be able to stomach what they say easier."

"What else have they said?"

Silence.

"Don't clam up on me now," she laughed nervously.

"I've been a harbor master for twenty-five years. Never in my life have I ever believed in stories of sea monsters or monsters in general. Whatever is going on on that island, it's going to be something big."

"Big bad or big good?"

"I honestly can't say for sure," Gerald stated. "Only time will tell."

Daisy suddenly felt uncomfortable. It was not Gerald's doing but rather the uneasy notion of what lay ahead.

Soon, the fog lifted, and the island came into view. The land stretched for what seemed like miles. There was no telling for sure just how massive it was or what kind of area it encompassed. She could see the white sandy beach as well as the loading dock. There were a few open slicks. The harbor master drove the ferry into one of them and began to lower the chain on the bow. Daisy was already in her bug by the time it dropped with a loud *clank*.

She drove off and up the cement road which was surprisingly clear of sand and dirt. Only having driven for a minute, she already felt at peace. The jungle sounds were wide in variety. Monkeys hollered and birds cawed as well as hooted. Eventually she came up to a gate which fenced off the whole area. A couple of guards patrolled the area.

One of them approached her. "Hello. May I see your credentials?"

The man's voice was deep. His stern expression suddenly made her feel anxious. "My what?"

"I need to see your credentials, ma'am."

"I was invited here."

"Are you Carol?"

"Who? No, my name is Daisy Conners."

"Then you may proceed."

The gate suddenly opened, and she drove through it without hesitation. Soon, she was nearing the visitor center. The path had narrowed a bit, but it was clear where she was given the signs that were on either side of the manmade path.

She stopped at the entrance. There was a large pair of wooden doors. Patience was eating away at her. Part of her began to wonder if she had come to the right island. The harbor master knew who she was. What if he took her somewhere she was not supposed to be? Questions were answered when the doors opened, and she became elated.

"Mom, Dad!" Daisy shouted.

Both her parents raced down the steps as she got out of her car. They quickly embraced.

Francis found it near impossible to break away, but he did and looked at his daughter. "You look terrific."

"How long has it been, sweetie?" Megan asked, still clutching her.

"Eleven months and eight days. But who's counting?" Daisy managed a chuckle.

"That's right. Saw you on your twenty-first birthday last."

Daisy beamed with excitement and admiration for her parents. It had been so long, and she had hoped they'd be around to see her for her twenty-second birthday. "I can't believe I'm here with you both."

"What do you mean, dear?" Megan asked.

"I was afraid I wouldn't see you for a longer time." She began to grow teary eyed.

Megan broke away. "Well. We're all here now. Let's show you around, catch up, and get some lunch."

"Sounds good to me," Daisy exclaimed. She then turned to her vehicle. "Need me to park anywhere specific?"

"It should be fine there. We don't open for another month." Francis smiled.

"Okie dokie! By the way, who's Carol?"

"Carol?" Megan looked to Francis, confused.

"It's just a code name the guardsmen use to verify who people are. If people say yes to the name Carol, then they cannot pass."

"Smart," Daisy chuckled.

The three then made their way inside the complex.

Outside, the visitor's center was alive with the sounds of the jungle. Inside, it was a wall of noise of construction. The hallways were being shaped into designs of some sort. Daisy could not be certain, but she could have sworn they resembled fossils. There was a fountain nearby that was babbling water through its cycling filtration unit. There were LED lights underneath that made the aquatic structure glow green.

"I feel like we haven't left outside," Daisy stated.

"This is only the beginning. Let's take you to meet the siblings first. I'm sure you'll understand the secrecy of this place soon enough," Francis said excitedly.

"The siblings?" Daisy raised a brow.

"Yes. Two professional hunter travelers. They helped track down several of the species we will have to showcase," Francis explained.

They approached an exhibit that was concealed by a pane of glass. The view window was ten feet high and twenty feet across. In the center, four feet or so above the ground, stood a man with his hands sticking inside some kind of contraption.

"Daisy, this is Peter Denning. One of the siblings I spoke of."

"Hello," she greeted him awkwardly.

He glanced over his shoulder. "How do ya do?"

"Uh, good. What are you doing there?"Daisy inquired.

"I can answer that," Francis began. "This place is not like any other in existence. It's not some theme park with a petting zoo. Saurian Safari is, quite literally, a trek through the easiest terrain imaginable. Yet you can still experience the enjoyment and thrills of the location and its inhabitants without running the risk of fatigue or injury."

There came a cracking noise from the foliage beyond the glass.

Francis continued. "We've traveled differently than other explorers and genetic scientists. We actually listened to the local legends of areas and followed several dozen guides until we came across one that led us to the exact location."

"... And what location is that?" Daisy said, without taking her eyes away from the view.

"Prehistoric paradise."

As if on cue, the enormous body of a spiked reptilian creature came out of the dense underbrush. Peter lifted his hands that were on the other side of the glass. They looked robotic. Daisy then realized they were extensions that acted as mechanical protection. He was holding up a large root that looked slimy. She nearly fell backwards. Her parents caught her.

"Is that...?"

"Yes, my dear," Francis smiled. "That is a stegosaurus."

"A dinosaur," Daisy muttered.

"I recognize that look," a woman's voice came from across the room.

She walked over and extended her hand. Daisy barely even registered the kindly gesture but managed to shake it nevertheless.

"My name is Sarah Denning. That big lug over there is my brother."

Daisy watched as Peter let the dinosaur take the root from him. It was a gentle process. The herbivore was careful not to bite the mechanical arms.

"It's so careful," Daisy exclaimed in amazement.

"The second layer of the arms provide an electrical shock that will shoot upwards if they bite through it."

"*They?*" Daisy looked perplexed.

"We have more than just this juvenile stegosaurus here," Sarah continued. "There are currently thirteen dinosaurs. Eight separate species. This here stegosaurus is our only herbivore." Backing away from the glass, the enormous animal marched back into the foliage. It then disappeared from view entirely.

"How big is its enclosure?" Daisy wondered.

"About the size of half a football field. We plan to expand when we introduce more species," Sarah explained.

"Where did you find them?"

Megan looked to her husband and smiled. She then returned her attention to their daughter. “We’ll show you.”

CHAPTER SIX

The tour continued.

Enamored by the park alone, Daisy could not feel more at home. She had traveled with her parents when she was much younger. Taking trips to Africa and Brazil, it became all too commonplace that nature was a force not to be reckoned with. The exotic locations were full of topography one would not find in the hustle and bustle of concrete jungles.

She remembered when she was twelve and she stumbled upon a captured primate. The chimpanzee was snagged in a weighted rope and hung suspended off the ground. She had managed to find her dad's utility knife and cut the ape loose. It turned to her and did something unexpected.

It had bitten her.

No scars or lasting injuries came of the act, but it had shocked her. She wondered why it attacked her when she had freed it. After a little pondering she deduced it was scared and unsure of who to trust.

Ever since then, she studied behaviors in animals and people more closely. She finally decided to take courses on the subjects. There were talks of becoming a therapist, but she wanted to specialize in all forms of life.

Now, as she walked under some overgrowth that hung from the metallic ceiling, she was reminded of where she stood in the world.

When they arrived at the next exhibit, a man stood by the glass just observing its contents.

"Oh, sweetie, this is Professor Alister Ward. He's the head of the carnivore division in the park." Francis nodded in the man's direction.

"Nice to meet you."

"Charmed," Alister said while not taking his eyes off the scene before him.

Daisy looked inside and saw that the room was very dim. "What's inside there?"

She turned to see Alister staring down her top. He quickly returned his gaze towards the specimens that were just now making enough movement to be seen by the naked eye.

"Utahraptor, three of them."

"What are they like?"

"They're the smallest carnivores we have on display. That being said, they stand about eight feet tall and are the ugliest bastards you'll ever see. Well… besides Ugros."

"Ugros?" Daisy tilted her head, confused.

"He's your next stop." Alister gave a creepy smile.

He then reached for a knob and turned it clockwise. The room before her began to light up. Inside became clear as day. They were tall animals for sure but the teeth were what terrified Daisy the most. They looked like triangular cylinders of death. Next were the claws. There were three with a fourth up on the ankle. It was like a bird's talon.

"Hideous," Daisy sneered.

"You haven't seen anything yet," Alister chuckled.

Daisy backed away towards her parents. "It was nice to meet you."

"Likewise." Alister watched her go.

He had not seen beauty like her since Megan came to him with her husband to hire him. He knew where Daisy's good looks came dominantly from. Smirking, he returned his focus to the creatures. They were getting a bit agitated with the light shining down on them, so he lowered the brightness back down to a reasonable luminance.

***

"I've all but given up," Jason Woo told a random scientist.

The man before him was busy calculating the measurements needed to feed Ugros. In Jason's opinion, they had been feeding him too much. He had come to Saurian Safari weighing 314 pounds. He was now pushing 380. While not grossly overweight, he was still big for his size. At six-foot-six and full of muscle, the humanoid was anything but appealing to the eye. He was completely bald and had some patches of green, scaly skin. His stomach was mostly a light shade of yellow.

At first, the team wanted to rename him Frog Man. Some even brought it up to Francis for a marketing tactic. Both him and Jason denied their request.

Ever since then, there'd been heated debates and cold shoulders in the lab. Jason suddenly became the outcast.

"We need to work together. This being needs to eat but he's gaining weight too fast. I told you to feed him less and yet he still gains and gains."

A technician turned to him. "We're injecting the right amount of fiber, calcium, and protein in his food. I don't know what else he could possibly need besides dietary pills and a good bath."

"I concur." The other scientist looked up from the lab setup. 'We can't keep doing this either. With all the carbs, he's become more aggressive. We still need to strike that right, healthy balance."

"I have someone who might be able to help." Francis appeared from around the corner suddenly.

Behind him was Megan and a young woman.

"This is my daughter, Daisy."

Daisy gave an awkward wave to the room. "Hey dudes."

Jason swallowed his frustration and held out his hand. "Hello. I'm Jason Woo. These are a couple of my staff members, Stanton and Grover."

Both men greeted her in unison. They had not been around much of the female staff. Sarah Denning was the only one who worked with the dinosaurs. The rest were hired waitresses. There had been another woman on their staff who worked with Ugros briefly but she had a family emergency that she could not ignore and had to leave early.

"Did I hear you say I can help in some way?" Daisy turned to her father.

"I think you can make a positive impact on this creature, yes." Francis smiled at her.

He then turned to Jason. "Take her to meet him."

Jason did as he was told and led Daisy over to the observation window. The room was mostly open with grass flooring and a small, muddy pond. There were two trees. One had a long overhang while the other went straight up with thick branches that only went out a few feet.

It was behind the first tree that she noticed something. A foot was sticking out. The humanoid sort of sauntered out into view in a casual, grumpy way. Daisy could not take her eyes off him.

He was mostly naked save for a pair of furry trousers. His forehead was enlarged and stuck out like a swollen mass. As he yawned, she saw teeth that were faintly yellow. There were a couple of rotted ones too. His eyes were pitch black and looked more like buttons on a doll than actual human eyes.

"What is he?"

Jason smiled reassuringly. "We don't know. Some cross between human and reptilian. Rest assured, he's smart like a human. Right now, he has the intelligence of a teenager or young adult. He can be quite moody."

She turned to face her parents. "The last ones we saw were way more hideous."

They both laughed.

"For the summer, would you be willing to work with him? Try to get him to cooperate with commands and such?" Francis asked.

"I think it's doable, yes." Daisy beamed with excitement. "This could be the career defining move I need to make."

"While we wanted to see you, we knew this would fit your job perfectly. Call it a double blessing." Megan grinned.

There was a pleasant silence between them, an unspoken cheer.

"While we're elated to have you on the team, I do think we should go over with you what we promised to," Francis stated.

"What? On how you found these creatures?" Daisy asked, intrigued.

"We'll start here." Francis approached the glass. "Ugros was found preserved in a caving system in Beijing. He was with another one of his kind. The two could not be more opposite."

"That's not an understatement," Jason continued. "Compared to Hysyr, Ugros is as docile as a sloth. He moves faster but doesn't harm anyone. We've had people go in the enclosure even on his off days. He pays them no mind. I'd say he's lonely, but he was cooped up with Hysyr for who knows how long."

"So then why would you need me?" Daisy asked.

"We need someone to teach him obedience and to help him understand human gestures and motions. A small step. We're hoping someday he'll even be able to talk," Grover said from the corner of the lab.

"One step at a time," Jason chuckled.

Daisy turned to her father. "So where did the dinosaurs come from?"

"That is actually an even simpler answer. The Congo."

"How far in did you have to go?"

"Not far at all. There have been expeditions to find hidden temples that have taken less time and resources. Sarah was told of a theory from one of the locals that I'm believing more and more. We push into the jungle, she pushes back."

"You think they were driven out of there by construction or something?"

"Or something," Francis confirmed.

***

Strong smells of a well-cooked meal loomed over the cafeteria. It would be another hour before dinner and Daisy decided to go unpack and freshen up. She undressed and stepped into the shower stall. It was a bit cramped, but it would do. She lathered herself with soap and washed her light brown hair.

The scent of freshness filled the bathroom. She was delighted by her new soap she was using. It had a fabric softener scent but was guaranteed to not cause skin irritation or dryness.

Eventually, she turned the water off and stepped out. Wiping the mirror with a cloth, she looked at herself. There was determination in her eyes. She had a sweet, girl next door persona about her but knew when to be strict with herself and others.

She had just demonstrated her capabilities with her friend. Not that she was all too pleased with herself when it came to her comments. She felt she had stepped too low even when being suggestive.

Getting dressed in a grey leopard print shirt and pair of light blue jeans, she made her way out of her room and down the hall. To her surprise, the dining hall was filled with people. There had to be at least ten from the science divisions and another ten from the security portion of the staff. A couple of waitresses were making their rounds, checking if people needed refills or to reassure them their orders were on their way.

Francis and Megan waved their daughter over and she motioned towards them. They were sitting with Jason Woo.

A young waitress came up to Daisy and handed her a menu. She left her to look it over before coming back to check what she wanted. She had decided on a side Ceaser salad and piece of meat loaf.

After the waitress left, Daisy looked to Jason. "So when can I begin working with Ugros?"

"Well." He finished swallowing a scallop. "Since you're only here for the summer, I suggest bright and early tomorrow morning."

He half expected her to groan. Instead, she nodded and smiled.

"The sooner the better," Daisy beamed with excitement.

A chair pulled out next to her. Alister took a seat. "Megan. We have to go over those results tonight."

Megan sighed. “I thought it could wait until tomorrow?”

“There’s new information,” Alister explained.

“Oh?” Megan feigned interest.

“I think it’s imperative.”

She groaned. “Alright. I’ll stop by after dinner.”

Daisy looked confused. Her mother took notice. “We work in the same lab.”

Before she could continue, a radio crackled on Jason’s hip. He unclipped it from his belt and raised it to his mouth. “Go for Woo.”

“It’s Denning,” Peter’s voice came over the radio. “We’ve got an intruder.”

CHAPTER SEVEN

The uninvited.

It was like a celebrity guest had arrived. Most of the guards were surrounding her as they trained their weapons at the ground before her feet. She stood defiantly. There was no hint of anxiety on her chipper expression. She oozed confidence and had a peppy nature about her.

Jason waded his way through the crowd. He did not like to be disturbed at dinner time and this took the cake for biggest distraction. Behind him was Francis who had a look of annoyance akin to Jason's. Daisy brought up the rear. Megan and Alister had gone back to the lab to look over the data.

"What are you doing here?" Daisy asked.

"You know this woman?" Peter pointed at her.

"Not personally, no. I know she's a reporter though. Catt something…"

"Brooke." She beamed a smile at her as if suggesting they were best friends.

"Did you follow me here?" Daisy asked.

Catt gave a sheepish grin.

"Whatever your reasons are for trespassing on this island, I can assure you, no reporters are allowed."

"I understand your position on the matter," Catt spoke in a kindly tone. "I'm not here to intrude on your privacy. I just wanted to have first dibs on opening day."

"Opening day is not for another two months," Francis scoffed.

"My paper wanted me to get here early. I can assure you; others will come and soon."

"And we'll ship them off just like we'll do with you." Francis gave the unspoken order and Peter grabbed her by the arm and guided her down to the docks.

As they made their way there, Catt noticed someone standing outside one of the buildings. He was smoking a cigarette and pacing back and forth, shaking his head. He looked familiar but she did not want to push further than she already had. It would just have to drive her crazy trying to place him for now.

When they got to the docks, there, a man on a little dinghy sat. He was not paying much mind to them. It was as if he knew this would happen.

Peter marched her down the grassy hill. The night air was cool as was the lawn.

"You're very pushy," Catt said.

"Sorry." Peter did not know why he apologized to her. She was trespassing on a private island. In his mind, he was surprised she was not imprisoned until the secret was officially out.

They arrived on the dock and Catt spun around and looked Peter in the eyes. "Maybe you'll be my next project."

She grinned and hopped onto the boat.

"What's that supposed to mean?"

Catt blushed. "Nothing insidious, I swear."

Peter watched as they drove away. He could not tell if she were flirting with him or attempting to use him in some capacity. He decided to not focus on it too much and made his way back up to the dining hall.

***

The next day, Daisy stood by the containment room door. She was a bit apprehensive about entering Ugros' enclosure. It was his domain, and she was intruding on it. Having mentally prepared all night for the encounter, she washed only the necessities and used organic soap. She was not sure how he would react.

"Are you ready?" Jason asked.

Daisy took a moment to reflect. This was her field. She knew how to deal with behavioral children and adults. Experience with autistic individuals was also in her criteria.

"I can do this," she not only told Jason and his team, but herself.

Stanton watched over the exhibit. Ugros was sitting by the murky pond water. He was playing with some weedy clump of plants. "He seems at ease."

Grover reached over and hit a button, and the door slid open with a mild swooshing sound.

Ugros heard it and turned in that direction. Daisy took one step inside, and he was immediately captivated. This woman was not like the others that had entered his new home before. She not only had an air of confidence, but she was remarkably beautiful. He stood his full six-foot-six height and looked down at her as she approached.

Daisy held out her hand cautiously. "It's okay, Ugros."

Her voice was sweet and calm. It reminded Ugros of another woman from a long time ago. It seemed like he had known her tone all his life. It was nurturing in a way.

Ugros immediately shrank in on himself and sat down again.

Daisy smiled pleasantly. "That's good."

Jason and his staff looked on in amazement.

"Looks like love at first sight," Stanton chuckled.

"That's what I am afraid of," Jason said.

Daisy continued towards the hulking humanoid. She knelt down next to him and held out her hand. He seemed scared.

"Everything's going to be alright."

Ugros leaned forward and sniffed her hand. It had a pleasant odor to it like a flower. He then let out a whining sound.

She smiled and pulled back slowly. She then began to walk away, leaving him in his vulnerable state. He looked as if he were contemplating what had just happened.

"That was incredible," Jason said as Daisy entered the lab once again.

"I don't want to intrude on him too much too fast. It's best we take this whole process slow," she explained.

"I agree," Jason told her.

"I'll stop by later. Can you get his vitals? I want a comparison between today's and yesterday's results."

"Yes, ma'am," Grover stated.

***

Daisy walked around the perimeter of the water fountain. The cobblestone was smooth and felt appeasing under her sandals. It was a relaxing place, able to bring about peace of mind. The dribbling water cascading into the surrounding circular enclosure was delightful to the ears. The wall of noise from staff barely even audible helped add to the fact that it was not barren like some long lost cave.

With that in mind, she began to think about Ugros. Pondering on his infantile like reaction to her opened the idea that he was nervous, shy, and maybe even attracted to her. She had not had the experience of many men who thought they were out of her league approach her with the suggestion of getting together.

When she first started college, her fellow sorority sisters would have practically laughed anyone like that off the campus. She never really gave into that mindset, instead opting to be accepting of anyone willing to be genuine with her.

The one and only type of guy that had approached her were preps. Her soft features and innocent aura made them see her as a virgin ready to be explored. They were half right.

Most of the sisters had abandoned her as a lost cause. Rebecca was that last strand attached to her, a string that needed clipping.

Thinking back to Ugros, he was an interesting specimen but nothing more. Even though she preferred the rugged look of mountain men, she could not see herself with a humanoid that seemingly had frog DNA intertwined within him. No one could confirm that just yet, but it was pretty obvious. Yet it was that innocent, worried expression he held that kept appearing in the front of her mind.

"You've watched Shrek too many times," she told herself as she made her way back to her room.

She passed Megan and Alister who were sitting in the cafeteria looking over some data. An unrelenting metaphysical pull made her want to sit with them. She was interested in just what was so important.

"I can't see why you had to interrupt me at dinner for this," Megan told Alister who was scratching his nearly bald head.

"You're not seeing it?"

"No," she replied with disdain.

Megan had been working with Alister for long enough. She felt it was time to either replace him or find someone else to work with him. He was brilliant when it came to herpetologists who specialized in carnivores, he was one of the best. She knew that did not make him the most revered but figured the most revered would draw too much attention. He needed to focus on his social skills more. It was clear as day that he was a flirtatious fool who spent little time thinking about others unless it was to ease his mind. Especially when it came to women and the concept of sex.

"Mind if I join you?" Daisy approached the table.

As far as Megan was concerned the meeting was over. Alister suddenly pushed the chair next to him. "Please. I'd love to get a second opinion on this."

Daisy saw the annoyed yet somewhat concerned expression on her mum's face. She did not want to be rude or make things awkward with anyone, so she accepted the invite.

Immediately, Alister spread a graph before her on the table. "You see these sharp inclines on the eighteenth of April."

She looked at the paper briefly. “Yes.”

“This diagram illustrates that the Utahraptor have been eating more regularly.” Alister then flipped to the next sheet. “Exactly one month later, their consumption amount dropped significantly only to increase a week later on May 27th.”

“That’s my birthday,” Daisy chuckled.

“Well, good thing you did not celebrate here. Because on May 27th, they nearly died,” Alister stated coldly. “They had eaten so much that we were afraid they’d go into some kind of food coma or just pass out.”

“A food coma?” Daisy’s eyebrow arched.

“It’s a theory he sticks by when it comes to dinosaurs,” Megan added.

“Okay?” Daisy’s voice trailed off.

“Regardless, I think they put off a week of eating because they were testing.”

“Testing?”

“That’s right.”

Daisy looked between them. “Testing on what?”

“On whether we’d go in the cage to examine them.”

“Are they that smart?” Daisy inquired.

“They’ve never shown that level of intelligence,” Megan continued. “They’re smart enough to live in a different environment than the Congo but so are the rest of the other species.”

“It’s not just a coincidence,” Alister stated.

“They were sick, Ward!” Megan spoke louder than she intended.

“Sick, ha! I think they were scheming.”

“Were there any signs that they were sick?” Daisy turned to her mother.

Megan looked down at the graphs. “Not to the naked eye, no. I wanted to run a few tests, but Alister warned me not to.”

“Why?” She turned to the man in question.

“Too risky. A smart predator knows when to lay in wait and when to strike. They don’t know how to pretend to be sick.”

Megan stood up. “This is ridiculous. I’m going to bed.”

She stormed off, fuming.

Alister turned to Daisy. “I think I made her mad.”

“She’s just hot tempered sometimes,” Daisy chuckled.

“I hope that doesn’t run in the family,” Alister chuckled nervously.

Daisy looked away to watch her mother go. In that brief time, she could feel Alister looking at her cleavage. She then stood up.

“Let me walk you back to your room.” Alister smiled like the Cheshire cat from *Alice in Wonderland.*

Again, Daisy felt compelled not to be rude, but she fought against it. "Maybe some other time."

"Okay," Alister sighed.

Daisy walked speedily away from the table. She did not bother looking back.

***

Captain Coleridge sat at the helm of his privately owned yacht that doubled as a research vessel. He felt content with running most of the operations aboard by himself. In this instance, he was in the company of a beautiful, buxom blonde scientist by the name of Patricia Ames.

Coleridge knew his marine biology colleagues were jealous that he got to work with her. She had the highest grade point average of any woman on the board and had looks unlike them too.

The high seas were usually a place most women of her glow would avoid. She was determined to see what the whales were up to in the Mozambique waters. She knew it was mating season and there would be a lot of activity.

"I hope we see some humpbacks. No pun intended," Patricia laughed as she held onto the guardrail.

He looked down at her from the helm of the ship. He was situated near the edge where the consol was. It was a rather small setup for such a decent sized vessel. There was no reason to complain though. It meant there could be only one person on the bridge at a time and that was how he wanted it.

"We should see some soon. We're coming up on the right area for their habitual sessions."

"Habitual sessions? Man, you guys need to get laid more," Patrica chuckled.

She then did something unexpected. She gave him a wink and a cheeky smile. The innuendo was right in his face and Coleridge was too shy to do anything about it. He reminded himself that he did not ask her to come but, rather, she signed up to do so.

Ever since I purchased this beast, the company has wanted to take hold of it for their own use. Coleridge thought about it some more. *Maybe that's why she's here. To try and butter me up.*

The thought made him visibly upset. He tried to mask it but was not doing so well.

"There!" Patricia called out.

He looked out and saw a massive humpback breach the surface and fall back down like a log. The plop was louder than it surfacing, he noticed. It then dove deep.

Both of them watched as it did not resurface. It was an awkward silence until it breached again five minutes later. This time, it was right in front of them.

Reacting as quick as a ninja on combat day, he spun the wheel left and the yacht turned hard to port. It then began to tilt further and further.

"Oh my god!" Patricia screamed repeatedly.

The boat teetered a bit further until it finally could not withstand the pull of gravity any further. Coleridge abandoned the wheel and reached for the survivor's kit he had clipped on the side of the consol. He then turned to his passenger. "Abandon ship! Jump as far out as you can."

Patricia did so as did Coleridge. They slipped under the waves, their bodies plummeting seven feet below the surface.

Coleridge surfaced first, just in time to see his prized boat sink beneath the surface. Patricia surfaced next.

"Are you okay?" he called to her.

"I think so."

Both swam towards each other. Before he could even react, something unexpected happened. She planted a kiss on his lips. When they parted, she looked at him. "I've wanted to do that all year."

He seemingly forgot about the boat at that moment. "Are you okay?"

"You already asked me that," she giggled.

A mournful cry could be heard as the whales began to sing. Patricia shuddered. "I can feel the vibrations under the water."

"Me too. But I don't think it's from the whale song."

Patricia looked back over her shoulder. "What about your boat?"

"My insurance will cover it," Coleridge said and then revealed his little boat before her. He opened it and pulled out a radio. Within minutes he reached the coastguard, and they said they would send someone out there and that they would be there within the next twenty minutes.

After he hung up, he looked at her. "A lot can happen in twenty minutes."

Without hesitation, she seductively swam up to him. She motioned close to him and fished out his privates from his swim trunks. She then slid them past her yellow bikini bottom and into her. They moaned in unison.

"I guess we've got to keep warm somehow," Coleridge said finally.

He then grabbed her and pulled her close to him. They began to rhythmically ride each other. It was not long before she felt an orgasm coming on. She looked up and moaned even louder than before. In that moment, she saw a dark shape in the sky.

"I guess they got here quicker than they said they would," she said.

Coleridge paid it no mind as he began to feverishly pound into her. "Oh, Patty."
She wanted to look down at him again but felt a sudden urge of panic. She examined the aerial craft further and realized there were wings attached. It was not a plane though, they were flapping.

"What the hell?"

Her body tensed up and not in a pleasurable way. It was enough to get Coleridge's attention who looked at her then followed her gaze.

"What is that?" she asked him.

"It looks like some kind of bird."

"That's a huge bird," she replied.

It then seemed to have noticed them as it was descending rapidly in their direction.

"Holy shit! Dive!" Coleridge screamed.

Before even getting a full view of the creature, he was already under the surface. When he was well over ten feet down, he turned and looked back. Saltwater stung his eyes, but he could have sworn he saw Patricia's body being yanked out of the water. He decided to return to the surface.

When he did, she was nowhere to be seen. He began to panic, sloshing around. It was not until a long object plummeted down next to him that he froze in fear. It was a severed leg with strands of sinew hanging out and the bone protruding from the stump.

CHAPTER EIGHT

A progression for the history books.

They met twice a day. Once in the morning and then once in the later afternoon. Daisy was always peachy and in a pleasant mood. She was patient with Ugros and, in turn, he showed signs of real understanding.

It had been a week since she first stepped into his domain and, already, the results were near fantastical. No one on the staff expected him to learn sign language so fast. The letters of the alphabet came to him so fast that he knew them within three days.

Now, Daisy was working on syllables. The sooner she could communicate with him, the easier her training would be. It was a step in evolution no one saw coming.

On day eight, Jason was busy with Stanton and Grover, discussing the future this humanoid could bring to science. Daisy took the opportunity with their backs turned and looked at Ugros. He returned the glance.

"I think you're special."

He grunted.

"You have a lot to provide. I think your progression is one for the history books." She turned to her piece of paper.

On it the word *Daisy* was written. She realized her name was close enough to Dad which was usually an infant's first word. It came out easier. She had been toying with the idea of having him say her name.

She then held up the note and said her name slowly.

Ugros did not pay much mind. He was busy staring at her.

"Don't look at me. Look at the paper," she giggled.

He gave a slight smirk. The way she laughed was appeasing to him. He then looked to the observation window. Knowing the consequences of even attempting to touch her would result in pain. He did not want to hurt her. Embracing her would make his life better.

The concept of love was somewhat lost on him. He had been with others of his kind, but they had just been for species survival. The mushy feeling inside him only arose when he saw her. He then turned to her again. He shook his head and then made his way over to the tree with the large overhang.

Daisy slumped into herself. She was making progress, but it was nothing beyond what a chimpanzee could do. She got up and made her way to the observation door. She swiped her authorization card and entered the room.

Alister was standing there with the others. They were discussing something but stopped when she entered.

"How's our friend?" Alister asked.

"He's fine."

"Good." He nodded.

"What's, uh, going on here?" Daisy asked.

"Hmm? Oh, nothing. Just chatting."

Daisy walked past them and out into the hallway. The sense of distrust she felt for Alister weighed her down like a ton of bricks.

"You really think this is a waste of time, don't you?" Jason asked Alister.

"I think our friend here is holding out. He knows more than he's letting on."

"Ha!" Stanton laughed. "I think you've been staring at the Utahraptor too long."

"Yeah! What, you think there's some secret dinosaur conspiracy going on?" Grover bellowed with laughter.

Jason hid his amusement well. "The way I see it, the good professor here is jealous."

"What!" Alister exclaimed.

"C'mon Ward. Wouldn't you rather have Daisy work with you than that big lug in there?" Jason teased him.

Alister scowled. "You're all a bunch of sick *bastards*!"

He then stormed out of the room of laughter.

***

Sarah stood in front of the Spinosaurus enclosure. Her eyes were glued not only to the animal but its habitat. The manmade swamp was ideal for this amphibious oddity. The giant sail on its back slid through the water. It appeared as a scaly fan slicing through it, trailing a ripple effect on either side. The water rushed by in a gentle motion.

This was her favorite dinosaur. The long snout and green eyes were what intrigued her the most as a kid. Now, it was the roar. It sounded like it was in pain and that pain enraged its fuel to hunt and kill.

A hunter with precision in its skill, it was a carnivore. Something else that was not known prior to its discovery in the land of the living was that it ate vegetation too.

When they discovered him, he was sifting through some weeds. They could not confirm if it was eating plant or the contents within for Alister had seen some crabs scurrying around it. She wanted to believe otherwise but part of her wanted to be wrong.

As a predator, having it eat plants would not only demoralize its level of ferocity but would allow for more dedicated carnivores to climb the food chain above it. At least, that was what she thought.

Peter was on the other side of the room, near the tyrannosaur pen. Its habitat was much different than that of the Spinosaurus.

It was a somewhat desert-like setting with dry trees, sand, and barren bushes. There was a small pit of water that was more mud than drinkable liquid. Still, the two adults and their one offspring did not seem to mind the habitat.

Unlike his sister, Peter did not have a favorite dinosaur. He admired them all but respected them from a distance. Only when capturing them did he ever even approach their personal space.

The hunt for them had been easier than he expected. There was truth to what Rocco had told them. The jungle was pushing back but Peter had suspicions.

Sarah came up behind him. "Learn anything new from staring at them?"

"Not really. They're brutes with the intelligence of a dude bro or football player."

"Ha!" she scoffed. "Maybe they'll learn more in a closed off environment."

Peter turned to her, dumbfounded. "When has that ever happened? No. They learn what they need to better in their own home than in some manmade contraption."

"I know. I was just kidding." Sarah held up her hands in mock defense.

The two stood in silence as they watched the female tyrannosaur approach the observation window. It studied them with an intensity that was punctuated by its dark red eyes. They seemed to stare into Peter's soul. He involuntarily shuddered.

"Hey, bro. Relax. She can't get you through there."

Without warning, the tyrannosaur rammed into the glass pane. It acted so quickly that neither had time to properly respond. Instead, they jumped back.

"I thought they could not see us through the window."

"Obviously, she's agitated by her own reflection," Sarah stated.

The dinosaur roared with a mighty rage. It was ear shattering on the inside; outside, it vibrated the frame and shook the wooden floor.

"My God." Sarah placed a hand on her brother's shoulder. "Are you hearing this?"

"I don't want to."

"She's obviously stressed about something."

Sarah then turned and almost froze in place. Shock rocketed through her very being and she felt her legs seemingly turn to Jell-O. It was not a common sight to see a Spinosaurus staring with deadly intentions at prey. A sight so startling, her hand fell from her sibling's shoulder and down his arm.

He turned to her. "What's wrong?"

At first, she could not answer. She finally found the confidence. "I think they are agitating each other."

Peter looked and saw the amphibious carnivore staring at them with an insidious expression. "Maybe they can see through the glass after all."

It was a long time before the dinosaurs broke apart. The staring competition ended but Sarah and Peter could not stop glancing back and forth.

"I haven't felt that uncomfortable since Alister tried hitting on me," Sarah said suddenly.

"Wait, what?" Peter snapped out of it.

"It was nothing," Sarah continued. "He asked to get some dinner and I rejected the offer. At first he didn't like that answer but when I told him 'tough shit' he got the hint."

"Man, that guy is weird."

"He just wants to be with someone. It just won't be me."

"I mean beyond that. He definitely has a funky smell."

"Ha!" Sarah started. "Not only that but he tends to just give off bad vibes. Like there's a darker side to him or something."

"Maybe he's got SDS," Peter suggested.

"SDS?"

"Small dick syndrome. It's enough to aggravate any man," Peter laughed.

"Men are weird," Sarah sighed.

"You'll only say that until you find a good one." Peter walked away.

"It won't be Alister. That's for damn sure," Sarah chuckled.

***

Francis sat at his desk in utter disbelief. The report had come in an hour ago that a yacht had been under attack by some unknown, flying creature and there was one fatality. The man who survived was barley speaking sense to most. Francis knew better.

He pulled out a chart of the area. Mozambique was approximately three hours from their location by plane. He feared a Pteranodon may have escaped and was heading to reclaim her flock. It was news he did not need at the moment.

Without thinking, he reached for his phone. After dialing the carnivore department, he waited as the phone rang. A familiar voice answered that sent a wave of relief over him.

"Peter. Listen to me. We may have a situation that I need you to check out."

"Oh?" Peter wondered.

"Bring yourself and Sarah to my office immediately."

"We'll be there, pronto."

They hung up.

Peter and Sarah entered the building with mixed feelings. They were not sure if they had been caught for something they had no idea had occurred or if there was a genuine problem that only they could solve.

They approached Francis who was standing near the secretary's desk. When they shook hands, it seemed formal. As if they had not seen each other for a while which was not the case. He seemed desperate.

"Let's talk in my office." Francis motioned towards the room in question.

The siblings were seated and began watching helplessly as their boss seemed to suffer from severe anxiety. His hands were shaking, and knees looked like they were about to buckle until he sat down.

When he did so, he looked at them with remorse. "I've just been informed that there has been an attack on a vessel not too far from here."

"An attack?" Sarah inquired.

Some sudden rain began to pelt the window next to Francis. The normally soothing sound seemed to startle him out of his skin. "I think it was one of the Pteranodons from Congo. It must have decided to investigate life outside the jungle further."

Sarah turned pale. "Rocco really was right."

"Come again?" Francis looked perplexed.

"Mother Nature has had enough. She's pushing hard now."

"Well, that's all well and good but people are dying. We can't be held accountable or even connected to the event that took place in Mozambique."

"It's that close?" Peter was shocked.

"I need you two to intercept it. Track it down even. There's no telling how much of an uproar this thing can cause. Especially since we're so close to opening day."

Sarah bit her tongue. She knew the zoo was at stake, but people's lives were as well. If they could stop it, it would cease worldwide panic.

"Where do you suggest we start?" Peter asked.

Francis slammed his fist onto his desk. "I don't know! You two are the hunters. You figure it out!"

They stared at him momentarily before getting up and making their way out of the room. Sarah turned to Peter. "We should have asked for overtime."

CHAPTER NINE

It was just like old times.

The decommissioned Bell UH-1 Iroquois sat in the middle of the field on the island. All it took was one phone call to Peter's old friends to get them out there. They had been ready and eager to go on a hunt since 2003 when they last went out to track a rampaging lion in Africa.

Bruce Canton stood in front of the others. He was battle-hardened and willing to take on more. He always welcomed new scars. Especially ones like the wound that ran down the length of his right cheek.

Behind him were brothers Golmer and Terrance Flintwood. If there were a more Southern pair of siblings, Peter did not know where to find them. Golmer was shorter than Terrance but built. Terrance towered over all of them.

Peter and Sarah approached them. It was like looking through one of their memory books – one where they were standing defiantly above the carcass of some predator, minus the dead animal. They had a look of determination on their faces. They weren't sure if Francis informed them on what they were hunting so a debriefing would be in order.

"I'm afraid there's no time to play catch up. We'll give you the scoop when we're on our way to our location."

Bruce nodded as did Terrance. Golmer looked confused.

"Erm, where are we heading?"

"Mozambique. Out on the water. Right where the humpbacks are mating."

"I guess we're in for a show," Terrance chuckled.

"You could say that," Sarah stated.

The five boarded the aircraft. Peter and Bruce were in the pilot seats. The rest were in the cockpit. Their flight was smooth for the most part. The occasional updrafts caused for recalculating the position of the helicopter. The rain was still coming down hard. It looked like buckets of water were being poured on the windows.

"Could've picked a better day to go huntin'. Just sayin'," Golmer chuckled nervously.

"No time," Peter said over the intercom. "We are to intercept a hostile, terrestrial organism."

"What, like a bird?" Terrance asked, his Cajun tone coming through thick.

"What you see here is to be kept top secret. In fact, when we get back, you are to sign non-disclosure agreements," Peter explained.

"Must be some big bird, huh?" Bruce said in his abnormally deep voice. He always talked slow which drove Peter crazy.

"It's not a bird so much as it's an avian reptile."

"A flying snake perhaps?" Terrance laughed. "Maybe a jumping jumbo alligator, I tell you what."

"It's not something you'd find on those hybrids of the week monster movies you two like to watch," Peter said with a hint of a smirk showing on his features.

"Then what is it?" Bruce asked.

"For starters, we think it's coming to attack the island. Hence why we need to intercept it."

"That island has always had a bad history," Golmer stated. "Is it still called Darken or does your boss not want to associate it with that in case of bad publicity?"

"The island doesn't have a name yet. At least as far as we know." Sarah looked out the window.

It was getting musky in the cabin of the helicopter, and she wished she could open the sliding door. She began to wonder when the last time the siblings bathed was.

"Either way, that island is bad news," Golmer said.

"What, like it's cursed?" Peter asked.

"Maybe sumtin' like that." Golmer placed his fingers near his mouth and patted them on his lips. "I think there're a lot of bad things that happen on that island. Enough to give it nicknames that aren't too pleasant like."

The five sat in silence for a bit. The wind began to pick up more and the whole aircraft began to shake. Metallic rattling could be heard.

"This is not ideal weather," Bruce stated.

"We don't have a choice. You may not like the weather, but that Pteranodon sure doesn't give a crap."

Bruce stared blankly at Peter. "Did you just say Pteranodon. You mean like the dinosaur?"

"They're not dinosaurs. They're flying reptiles that just so happened to be around during the time of the dinosaurs," Sarah corrected him.

"So… a dinosaur?" Bruce gave a hearty chuckle. "I can't believe I got out of bed on my day off for this."

"You have us chasing those things that Ray Harryhausen used to make stop animation puppets for?" Golmer laughed.

"I think I saw them on one of those hybrid monster movies of the week not too long ago actually," Terrance added. "I think it was called a Piranodon or something stupid like that."

"Listen! This is no joke!" Peter shouted. "It's already taken one human life as far as we know. It could've taken more by now. We need to stop it."

"Bad publicity. What'd I say," Golmer chuckled. "Did it escape from the island?"

"No. But it's close enough to be a concern."

"What exactly is on that island of yours, Pete?" Bruce asked.

He did not answer.

"We're cloning reptiles for our private zoo."

"Don't ya mean dinosaurs?" Terrance was cackling now.

"No. Just normal reptiles. Only of the much bigger variety. Think of twenty foot Komodo dragons and you'll see what I mean."

"So why is there a dinosaur, I mean, flying reptile heading towards your island?" Bruce asked.

"We found eggs in the Congo. They haven't hatched yet, but I think they belong to mama out there."

"Speak of the devil," Peter said suddenly.

Bruce stared in disbelief as Terrance and Golmer motioned to the front of the helicopter.

"No fucking way," Bruce said coldly.

"Look at the size of that thing." Golmer swallowed hard.

"Battle stations, pronto. You all know what to do!" Peter shouted. His voice boomed over their headsets, snapping them out of their amazement.

Terrance was the first to duck back into the cockpit and load his gun. Sarah was already back there and ready. Golmer could not take his eyes off the animal.

"We're going to kill it?" he asked.

"No, we're going to make friends with it," Peter said sarcastically. "Of course we're going to kill it."

It was clear the avian predator spotted them for its head snapped in their direction. As it flapped its wings aggressively, it pushed through the rain and closed the gap between them.

"Evasive maneuver!" Bruce screamed frantically.

Peter tilted the aircraft to the left just as the Pteranodon soared past them. Sarah slid the door open and opened fire just as it passed by. There were a few hits but nothing that would cause long term injuries.

"It's like a carnivorous canary!" Golmer shouted as he opened the door adjacent to Sarah.

He and Terrance aimed their guns outside, peering over the edge. The rain was coming down even harder and the wind was becoming unbearable. The constant pelting of rain and gusts of harsh air made them squint their eyes slightly.

"C'mon out, you ugly birdy!" Terrance screamed.

There were no signs of it. No massive, organic object flew by to peck at them.

"Where is it?" Peter shouted.

"I don't have eyes on it!" Sarah called out.

"We don't either," Golmer said, speaking also for his brother.

"I think I scared it off," Sarah said.

She then placed her machine gun down and turned back towards the chairs. She pulled out a case, opened it, and carefully unsheathed her compound hunting bow. She retrieved some arrows and returned to her station.

"There it is!" Terrance cried out.

He and Golmer both spotted it as it hid behind the clouds, its massive silhouette barely visible. It screeched in pain and then dove downward towards the sea. The siblings stopped firing right before the skids under the helicopter.

"Someone needs to get eyes on that! Now!" Peter shouted again.

Some clouds began to move in an abnormal way. Something broke through them so fast that no one had time to react. The Pteranodon burst upward and snatched onto Terrance's leg. With a mighty twist, it was broken. Then, with another tug, it came off. It all happened so fast that Golmer did not have time to fire his weapon at the beast.

"Ahhhrrgh!" Terrance cried out in pain.

The Pteranodon swiftly swallowed the leg and then charged again for some more. Golmer was too busy trying to pull his brother to safety to notice. The hulking reptile's head practically crashed into the cockpit. It snapped at them with its long cone-shaped beak. Sarah was quick to position herself and managed to pull the arrow out of the quiver and position it on her bow. She pulled back and let loose the arrow. The sharp thwacking sound was barely heard over the rain, wind, and rotors. Still, it found its mark directly in the creature's left eye.

Screeching in utter agony, the Pteranodon slipped out and fell away from the Bell UH-1 Iroquois. It plummeted down into the sea with a tremendous splash.

"Did ya get it?" Golmer cried out while cradling his brother in his arms.

Sarah took a deep breath. "I got it."

The flight back was the most awkward one Peter had ever had with his friends. There was an unspoken anger with each of their glares. They arrived at the Cape Town hospital and Terrance was carted off on a gurney into the emergency ward.

"Will he be alright?" Sarah chased after one of the doctors, but they closed the door in her face.

Peter sat down in a brooding state. He did not want to face Golmer but realized he had to. He got up, made his way over to the water dispenser and poured himself and Golmer a cup before making his way over to his friend.

"Thirsty?" he asked.

Golmer did not act out like Peter thought he would. Instead, he just shook his head.

"Was it worth it?" Bruce spoke up from the other side of the waiting room.

Turning to him, Peter saw that Bruce was a shell of his former self. They had all been best buds back in their glory days. They would die for each other. Now one of them may die because of him. He did not know how he would be able to live with his decision.

Sarah turned to Bruce. "Don't start anything. We still need to come up with a reason."

"A reason!" Golmer shot up from his seat. "A reason for what?"

"We can't tell them in good conscience and morality that he was attacked by a bird," Peter continued. "Looked more like a jaguar attack to me. Wouldn't you say so, sis?"

Golmer turned to Sarah. "Say what you feel."

Sarah could tell he was seething and ready to sever the friendship between them right then and there.

"I think we need to sleep on it," she suggested.

"There's no sleeping on it. He was attacked by a flying monster!" Golmer raised his voice.

Everyone in the waiting room, including nurses, turned to him.

"Keep quiet!" Peter snapped. "We're all in shock over what happened."

"Go to hell, Pete." Golmer motioned over to Bruce and grabbed him by the collar. "I need a drink."

The two made their way out of the hospital and outside.

"Maybe we should go after them? They didn't sign the agreement." Peter was about to run off after them.

"Don't," Sarah began. "No one will believe them, and they know that. Let's just focus on retrieving the carcass."

"Why bother? It's probably been fed on by every little nibbler in the sea."

Sarah glared at him. "For closure, Pete. Seriously, just humor me."

The two headed out and grabbed a taxi. They knew they weren't getting a ride on the Huey back to the island.

As the siblings stood on the side of the street, waiting for a cab, she watched them. She wondered why they were there, all the way from Darken Island. Of all places at a local hospital. Her mind raced with possibilities. Was there an accident at the resort on the island? Could there be an epidemic from what they've created, and they've come to warn doctors and nurses to be prepared? She realized the former was more likely.

She carefully crossed the busy street. "Hey strangers!"

It took a moment for them to recognize her. "Ms. Brooke?" Peter inquired.

Her luscious locks of brown hair bounced as she skipped across the road. He had to say to himself that she was bad news. There was nothing for him to gain with reporters.

"Please, call me Catrina." She stopped before them.

"We are not talking with you," Sarah said with a cold demeanor.

"Is everything alright?"

"Yes. Now please go away," Sarah demanded.

"No, wait," Peter said suddenly.

"What?" Sarah glared at her brother.

"I think she can be of some use to us. Or at least, to shed some light on a previous incident."

"What are you going on about, Pete?"

"Catrina, did you hear about the yacht that was attacked?"

"Who hasn't?" she giggled.

"Well, we know what did it."

Her eyes opened wide. “Please, do tell.”

“What are you doing?” Sarah stared daggers into him.

“Firstly, they were not attacked by some flying creature. It was actually quite the opposite. There was an accidental cargo that dropped from a helicopter. It landed on the boat, destroying it. Whatever happened to the woman, I can’t say. Shark maybe.”

Sarah looked at Peter in disbelief. Catrina noticed her glare and realized there was more to the story.

“We were sent to retrieve the cargo. One of the men was injured in the process. Hence why we’re now here at the hospital.”

“What was in the cargo?”

“I don’t know. It was top secret materials from the Navy.”

“So, this has nothing to do with your island or resort?”

“We just happened to be nearby and accompanied them out to retrieve it. We’re friends of theirs.”

“Where may I find these pilots?”

Peter pointed at the bar across the street. “Hurry. You might want to get them before they become too plastered to make any kind of sense.”

Catrina smiled. There was a hint of uncertainty, but she ran with it. She then marched over to the bar.

“You’re a cold son of a bitch!” Sarah pushed him in the shoulder.

“What’s your deal?”

“They’re our friends! You just put the blame on them!”

Peter remained silent.

“Why? All so you could try and nab some news reporter poontang?”

“Hey! I’m just looking out for the resort and Francis. Remember, they didn’t sign anything.”

“You’re such an idiot! What if we need their services again? Did you even think about that?” Sarah practically screamed.

Again, Peter remained silent.

“Stop thinking with your dick and start using your head!” Sarah stormed off.

Peter slowly followed.

***

“I can’t believe you used to date her.” Bruce looked over at his bar buddy and chuckled. “You must’ve been desperate.”

Golmer did not show any hint of humility on his face. Instead, he looked at his drink and began to sulk. “I can’t believe this is happening.”

"It's a lot to process," Bruce said in his low, dimwitted voice. "A flying reptile attacked us, nearly killed your brother, and now we've learned who we can really trust in this world."

"I guess so." Golmer knocked back his shot glass and returned it to the table with a slam.

"Is this seat taken?" A woman stood there before them.

Bruce, like he did with all women who even gave him attention, began to sweat profusely. Golmer on the other hand relished in the idea of hooking up with some random chick. It would help get his mind off the situation at hand.

"No."

"My name is Catrina Brooke. You can call me Catt," she explained as she took a seat next to Bruce.

In that formal instant, Golmer realized this was not a social call. "What do you want?"

"Well, for starters, I'm a reporter. I heard about your trouble this afternoon."

"Who told you?" Golmer asked.

"Peter Denning."

"Has the bastard finally grown a conscience?" Golmer thought and said aloud.

Catt paused momentarily. She wanted to approach this as delicately as possible. There was something off about the whole ordeal and she did not know who to believe just yet. "Care to tell me your side of the accident?"

"Accident? Lady, the only accidents were my brother getting nearly killed and us ever trusting Peter to begin with."

"What happened out there?"

"Oh, he didn't tell you?"

"Tell me what? He referred to the cargo falling onto the yacht."

"Ha!" Golmer scoffed loudly. "No. We were attacked, Ms. Brooke, by a fucking prehistoric bird!"

CHAPTER TEN

There was no wasted time.

Daisy Conners found herself down in Ugros' enclosure more times than not. She only went to her room to sleep or wash up. It had been nearly two weeks since she arrived and, already, she was fascinated by him. His intelligence was remarkable as was his cautiousness.

As she entered his domain again, she could feel the heat had been turned down. Summer was now in full swing, and the heat was bearing down on the place, turning it into an industrial microwave. She saw Ugros sitting on a log near the pond.

When she first started, she was extremely wary of him. He was a hulking brute after all. Though he looked intimidating, it was clear he would not harm a fly. She approached him without worry this time. He turned and saw her, giving a toothy smile.

"Hello there." She patted him on the shoulder.

He moaned with relief. She sensed that he missed her and was only sitting there to await her return. She found it endearing yet also romantic in a way. He was genuinely ecstatic to see her and not in a lustful way. At least, as far as she could tell.

"How are you today?"

He nodded.

Showing signs of understanding human language was amazing and all. Talking was just out of reach for him at the moment though. It was not from a lack of trying. He would try to form words to the best of his capabilities, but it only came out as grunts.

She turned and saw Jason looking over the computer set up in front of the viewing window. The two of them had come to an agreement that Ugros was able to be trusted.

After a few minutes, Jason left the room. It was empty. Stanton and Grover had taken the day off. The jungle sounds coming from the monitor still played and Daisy felt like she was out in the wild. She took a seat next to Ugros.

"You're very special. You know that?"

Ugros nodded again.

Daisy shimmied closer to him. "Listen. I can tell when someone likes me."

He looked to her, saddened, as if he were caught red handed and was going to be in trouble.

"There's nothing wrong with that." She smiled. "I think we should just keep this professional. I have a lot at stake. As do you. I wouldn't want either of us to have any problems."

With a carefully raised hand, Ugros touched her cheek. She let out a single tear and he wiped it away.

"I hope you understand."

Again, he nodded.

***

Jason entered the empty mess hall. It would not be that way for long since lunchtime was rolling around. He took this opportunity to make his way over to the food court. He approached a place he despised, Jane's Juice Jamboree, and sat on one of the four swivel chairs.

The owner of the establishment, Aly Jane, motioned towards him. "Hello Mr. Woo. What can I get for you today?"

"Hmm. Not sure. I may need a minute."

"Take your time, darlin'." Her Texan accent was laid on thick.

Despite growing up in East Asia, he always had a sort of kinship with the Wild West. He liked to watch the John Wayne, Gary Cooper, Clint Eastwood classics. That Southern drawl was one he always admired. Especially when it came from a pretty little thing like Aly Jane.

When she returned a few minutes later, she asked the same question. He gave a similar response.

She did not seem agitated or annoyed. Rather she was a patient soul.

"Jane!" he called her back over.

"Yes, Mr. Woo."

"No need to be formal. You can call me Jason." He smiled.

She grinned at that. "Okay, Jason. You can call me Aly."

"Alright Aly, I'm ready to order."

She held up her pad of paper. The décor of Jane's Juice Jamboree had a 50's aesthetic. It was very charming. Everything from their uniforms to the pens with the fluffy tops that were used to jot down people's requests. It was very stylish.

"Hours."

"Hours? I'm not sure what you mean?" She whipped a lock of strawberry blonde hair out of her eye.

"I want to know what your hours are?"

"Oh." She laughed. "We open at eight and close at six."

"I see. Can I come back at seven?"

She gave a perplexed look. "Why would you want to come back at seven?"

"So, I can take you out on a date."

Her face blushed so much that her whole face turned beet red. "Oh, I, um."

Standing there with the question hanging in the air, she thought it over.

Kaboom.

Both their heads snapped in the direction of the noise.

"They're still doing construction on the garden?" Jason asked.

"It's turned into a big dust bowl out there." She sighed. "I hope it'll come out okay. Those machines have been driving me crazy."

Jason peered out the window. There was an excavator, forklift, and bobcat truck. "You would think they're building a new shopping mall."

"Maybe," she said with a wry smile. "How does 6:30 sound?"

He turned to her. "Sounds perfect."

***

Jason had arrived early at the café. Aly was just closing up when a last-minute customer arrived. It was one of the other staff who worked in the restaurant.

"Hey, beautiful," he began. "Been staring at you across the dining hall all day. How's 'bout you and I go back to my bungalow? I'll offer you a drink of my best wine?"

"Sorry, Lester, I already have a date." She pointed to Jason who was sitting at the table.

"Oh." Lester approached Jason's table.

He looked like he was about to start something when he simply walked by him. "My apologies, sir."

"No worries," Jason said.

"Okay, just give me five minutes." She beamed with excitement.

Jason nodded.

It was four minutes later when they were making their way out of the dining hall.

"I hope you're not going to take me back to your bungalow?" she giggled.

"Ha! I just figured we could go for a walk."

"Sounds good to me." She held out her hand and he happily took it.

They ended up at the wishing fountain near the entrance. He fished out a quarter. "I wish this night would go horribly." He tossed it in.

"Why'd you say that?" she asked.

"Because if you say your wish out loud, it won't come true." He smiled at her.

She laughed. "You're cute."

"It's just my eyes."

"Don't say that! That's awful!" She could not help but laugh harder.

"We all look alike." He then opened his eyes wide with his fingers. "Even when we try to be American."

"What nationality are you?" she asked between chuckles.

"Thai. Although my mom's side of the family is from Germany."

"Interesting combo." She smiled.

"Yeah, one hundred percent."

The two then began to walk aimlessly.

"It sucks it's raining out," she said.

"Hopefully the storm passes before the trial period."

"The trial period?"

"Yeah," he began. "A bunch of investors are coming to the island later this week. I'm sure they'll go over it with you. It's not for another three days. Friday, to be more accurate. Anyway, they'll come and hopefully show potential interest."

"I think we can wow them."

"No doubt." He smiled at her.

They sat in silence briefly.

"Can I ask you something?" she inquired.

"What's up?" Jason turned to her.

Aly paused for a moment, thinking over her question. It was a bit risqué given the progress of the park. Still, she needed to know. "Is it safe?"

"Is what safe?" His eyebrow arched.

"The park. I mean, I know it's state of the art but... *Is* it safe?"

Jason smirked. "I wouldn't be here if I didn't have complete faith in the Conners' vision." He took a deep breath. "I work with Ugros closely but I also worked with Hysyr. The two were complete opposites."

"I'm sorry. Who and who?" she giggled.

"The humanoids that will be on display."

"Oh, I heard something about them!" she exclaimed. "Aren't they like frogmen or something."

"Or something." He smiled warmly at her. "Hysyr was as aggressive and unpredictable as a crocodile, while Ugros has all the compassion of a domesticated chimpanzee or canine."

"Really?"

"Yes, and when the Conners came, I was certain they were going to want Hysyr. Instead, the saw the red flags and opted for Ugros. I know they're playing it safe."

"Well, that makes me feel better," she said sincerely.

They continued down to the exhibits. Down the hall were the beginnings of a jungle environment with faux leaves and trees. The area was not too constricting. It was easy to navigate through.

"Let me show you one of my favorite dinosaurs," Jason said as he led her towards a glass pane. "The Dilophosaurus."

He looked inside and saw that the two of them were sleeping, nestled next to each other in the corner on a bed of straw. On top of their heads were a pair of dark red, arched crescents. Their needle-like teeth were visible on the top jaw but the lower portion was shorter and did not stick out as much.

"They look so peaceful," she smiled.

"Yeah, don't let them fool you. They're carnivores like ninety percent of the species here at Saurian Safari."

"You sound like a tour guide," she chuckled.

He smiled wryly at her. "Follow me and I'll take you to the Baryonx enclosure."

She giddily took his hand and the two continued their venture into the park.

***

It was as if he'd never left. Peter stormed through the jungles of Borneo as he made his way to the river. By his side were Bruce, Golmer, and Terrance. They were the last in the line of great, white hunters in the area for the season. They had picked the perfect time to come. A giant saltwater crocodile had been terrorizing a village and there had been many casualties. A regular Gustave.

Just in time to have missed the rainy season, the four men marched onto the dock whose pilings were barely even holding it together.

"So much for standard issue," Terrance chuckled.

They piled onto the boat. Bruce was aft, manning the engine. Golmer and Terrance were situated in the middle while Peter was at the bow. They sped through the water knowing full well where the beast was likely situated.

Water brushed past the hull and it sprayed upward, splashing Peter repeatedly. He paid it no mind. It felt refreshing in the sweltering heat.

It was a scenario they had hunted through many times before. A predator terrorized a village, and they were sent in to stop it. Last time was a lion in Africa. This time presented a bit of a challenge. Each one of them secretly prayed that the crocodile was ashore on a sand bank.

There was a *thwomp* which made all their attention turn to the water.

"It's under us!" Terrance cried out.

Golmer checked the other side but found no signs of the crocodile. The water was somewhat clear which made for easier visibility.

Everyone but Terrance agreed that it must have been a log. He was still on edge, fidgeting in his seat on the starboard side. It was as if his fears greeted him personally when a hungry set of jaws shot outward and snagged him in the crocodile's toothy maw.

Peter was the only one to see it happen. "No!" he cried out.

"No!" Peter shot up in bed.

Faint pelting rain could be heard as the storm passed overhead. It trickled down the windowpane of his cottage.

He looked around in the room but, besides the glow of moonlight that poured in from the outside, the room was dark. A sinking feeling came over him. The blackness of parts of the room resonated with his very soul. A match made in color.

"What have I done?" Peter placed his hands over his face and wept.

After that, he decided he was not going to get any sleep. He climbed out of bed and made his way over to the bathroom. The sink was marble and looked fancy which was offset by the teak closets below. He washed his face and then made his way out of his room and down the hall.

The Utahraptor enclosure was first up. He was taken aback to not see Alister there but rather Sarah. He walked up to his sister who was observing the dinosaurs in the dim darkness. Her eyes lit up when she saw Peter's reflection in the glass window, and she spun around.

"Can't sleep?" she asked.

"No," Peter said with a stale expression.

"Me neither." She turned back to face the exhibit.

"Had a nightmare," Peter stated.

Sarah ignored what he said. "You ever wonder why animals of some shape or form always survive and evolve except for one kind?"

"Let me guess, you're going on one of your speeches about evolution?"

"Human beings are a disease. An ailment that has wretched this planet low of resources. Now, things like what happened to Terrance today occur and we're left feeling guilty after the fact," Sarah continued. "The thing is, Pete. Animals don't feel guilty. They just survive without destroying themselves or the planet. We push too much and, therefore, will be the cause of our own destruction."

Unbeknownst to her, her brother was trying to take what she said seriously. It was that antagonizing bond they shared that constantly got in the way of their genuine heart-felt exchanges.

"So, what do we do now?" he asked.

"For one, I think you need to make up with Golmer and the others. What you did was despicable."

"Okay, and then what?"

"Then take a good look at yourself and maybe you'll find out just what you are."

"And what's that?" Peter smirked.

"I'm not you, I can't say."

"Now wait a minute, wait a minute. You went through that entire speech only to leave me on a cliffhanger?"

"I don't expect you to understand. Just call Golmer and soon."

"I doubt he'll even pick up."

"Maybe he will. You're assuming the worst."

Peter made his way next to her and pressed against the railing. They looked in the exhibit. Sarah saw the yellow eyes staring back at them. All Peter saw was himself, reflecting off the glass.

CHAPTER ELEVEN

Dreams of screams.

Alister Ward, unbeknownst to his fellow scientists and coworkers, had an obsession. It was one he could not shake no matter how hard he tried to tell himself it was wrong. There was just something about it. The sound was enticing, even gratuitous. The unbelievable magnitude some could achieve was impressive.

The noise was as shrill as a tea kettle whistling yet more guttural. He had only seen human women do it in movies and on television. Their cries of either excruciating pain or fear just tickled his fancy. There was no other way around it.

On a Wednesday night, in the mess hall, he found Daisy Conners eating from a cup of ice cream. He decided to join her. He would not ask. Just pull up, sit next to her. Make himself comfortable. He knew he would not do anything, but that closeness could only bring him within inches of a possibility. He almost laughed at the notion. Still, he had to try.

"Hey there." Alister pulled up a chair and plopped down in it.

"Oh. Hi," Daisy feigned interest.

"How are you doing?"

"I'm fine." She dug into her cup for more ice cream but was disappointed to find none. She sat back and sighed.

"Are you sure?"

"Yep."

"Well. Good. I didn't want to catch you at a bad time." Alister cleared his throat. "I was wondering if, maybe, you'd like to have breakfast with me in the morning?"

"For what?"

Oh, she can only play aloof for so long. Alister grinned from ear to ear. "I want to talk to you."

"What about?"

"Oh, this and that."

Daisy turned to him. The lustful old man's smile was creepy. His red lips stuck out of his pale, wrinkly face as if he were a clown. She hated clowns.

"I'm sorry. I'm skipping breakfast tomorrow. I've got to work with Ugros on some stuff."

She stood up.

"I'm starting to have suspicions," Alister stated suddenly.

Daisy froze in place.

"Maybe we should just chat right now."

"About what?"

"Oh." He cocked his head to the side. "This and that."

"I'll take a rain check." Daisy turned and practically ran out of the mess hall. All Alister could do was smile insidiously.

***

Morning arrived as did a thick fog. There was poor visibility as far as the coastline and several miles out to sea. It was a peaceful time of day with tropical birds chirping and cawing. The summer air was a reasonable seventy-four.

Francis rolled over on his bed and kissed Megan on her head. She was still fast asleep after working in the lab until the wee hours of the morning. All she could do now was groan.

"Rise and shine, honey."

Megan barely moved. All she did was emit a low groan.

"C'mon, honey. The investors arrive tomorrow. We've got lots of work to do." He patted her rear. "Time for sleep later."

Megan finally came around and looked at Francis. Her eyes were a bit dry and crusty but, to Francis, she still looked twenty years old.

"Put on some fresh coffee." She smiled.

"You've got it." He was about to get up but stopped. "Say, how about a quickie."

She chuckled. "I thought you were in a hurry?"

"Well. We have half an hour before we go see Daisy and Ugros. I think we can fit it in."

"Go ahead. You do whatever you want. All the while, I'm going to catch up on some rest."

Francis didn't know what to say. He had never had intercourse with his wife unconscious. Still, he needed to release some stress and Megan needed to relax. It was probably for the best.

To his surprise, by the time they were done, it was not a challenging experience. Rather rewarding. She even moaned a few times which he was not sure if she would. He finished and went into the bathroom and was about to get into the shower stall.

"Hey!" Megan called to him.

"Yeah?" Francis peeked his head around the corner.

"You forgot to put the coffee on." She smiled.

***

It was the first of two big days for Daisy. She had to showcase Ugros' progress and her ability to train him. She knew her skill sets had aided her in her successes when it came to him but she wanted to be exemplary.

The show started at nine o' clock on the dot and yet her parents, Alister Ward, and the team in charge of Ugros were in the viewing room ten minutes early. She knew that Ugros was a bit of a diva but decided to rouse him out of his slumber early. It would be another way she could show how well trained he was at following commands.

Walking further into the enclosure, she made her way over to him. He was resting under some shade provided by a tropical tree she was not familiar with. There were ferns surrounding him, obscuring the humanoid from the crowd. She had never been in there. It was Ugros' home away from home.

Ting. Ting. Ting.

She rang a little bell, and the brush began to sway. Ugros came lumbering out.

"He's grown," was the first thing Francis could think to say.

"He's nearly seven feet tall," Jason stated.

"It's only been…" Francis tried to do the math in his head.

"One month and four days since your last visit," Grover smiled.

"Show off," Stanton scoffed.

"I think it has to do with his environment. You know, how snakes can grow as large as their containment," Megan suggested.

"That's actually a myth," Jason began. "We think it has to do with the change in temperature. His cave was not exactly paradise. Perhaps the heat makes him grow."

"Fascinating." Francis stared at Ugros in wonderment. "How large do you think he'll grow?"

"Can't say for sure," Jason said.

"Maybe you should change the temperature," Megan said. "We don't want him having any muscle or bone issues."

"I would have agreed but his containment is currently at seventy-five. Making it colder may cause him discomfort. Or at the very least make him want to hibernate."

"Not good for shows," Francis added.

"Exactly." Jason returned his attention to the show.

Daisy had already made Ugros sit and now he was playing patty cake with her. She then told him to say her name. He stumbled a bit, desperately trying to form the word with his thick lips.

"You can do it." She gave him a warm smile.

"D, Dnnnn," he stammered.

"You got this."

Ugros took a deep breath and sighed. He looked at her with an admiration he had never encountered before. Her whole face glowed as did the smile behind it. She smelled so sweet. He just wanted to act on his animal instincts. Others of his tribe had taught him to resist these urges. There were other, more important matters. At that time, they were being hunted by a pack of tall, bipedal reptiles. Most were slaughtered besides him and one other who had turned sour and feral towards him.

He could not remember how long ago it was. Only that it looked much different than the here and now. His tribe spoke in grunts. He had watched as his father fought off the terrible lizards with the other hunters. He was in charge of looking after his mother. They watched from a high vantage point.

His father fought valiantly. He was the last one standing and, therefore, became an easy target. They watched in horror as the giant carnivores tore him apart.

Before long, they found a cave where another one of their tribe was. He ushered them in, but they did not get far. A pack of smaller, more ferocious creatures charged and tore his mother apart.

Ugros did not remember how but there was a landslide and he and the other humanoid were trapped in the cave. It froze over many years while they hibernated.

Now he was looking at Daisy. The most beautiful thing he had ever seen, and he was having trouble trying to speak her language to please her.

"Dnnnaaa."

"You've almost got it!"

No matter how much he tried, he could not pronounce the second letter.

"That's okay." She patted his shoulder. "You did great."

Alister was turning red.

Stanton took notice. "What's the matter, Doc? Jealous of the frogman?"

He and Grover laughed as Alister spun on his heel and stormed out.

"What was that all about?" Francis inquired.

Megan scooched closer to him. "I'll find out later."

After the show, Daisy entered the viewing room to a resounding applause. There had been no hint of how much had been accomplished with Ugros. Daisy had kept it a secret from everyone besides Jason. Not even Anton, nor Grover had known how far she had come. Sure, it was a small step, but a large one at the same time. He was learning to speak, and he obviously followed commands.

"I wonder how well he'll listen to another instructor?" Anton wondered.

Daisy felt obligated to Ugros. He was the most sensitive individual she had ever met, and, in that, he had a lot to learn. Someone less patient might undo everything she had worked so hard on.

"I'm not going anywhere," she said suddenly.

"What?" Francis looked at her with confusion.

"I don't want to go back to college and deal with all the drama and excruciating work they provide." She took a deep breath. "I'll stay and work with Ugros. He needs me and, in a way, I need him."

No one said a word for a length of time that was uncomfortable. Finally, Francis stood up and walked up to her. He embraced her, giving her a tight hug, reminiscent to when she was a child.

"This is great news!" Francis cheered.

"Agreed!" Megan smiled warmly.

"You can be Jason's part time assistant."

Daisy nudged him. "Daaad."

"Okay, okay. You can be Jason's *full-time* assistant to aid him with Ugros."

***

Alister stood in front of the readouts which were displayed on a computer monitor straight out of the 1990s. There were strange signs and symbols that were being utilized to feed the information into his file. It would only take a few minutes.

Time elapsed at a snail's pace. The transfer reached 98% when he heard the door shut behind him. He cursed under his breath but remained calm. He knew it was Megan coming to talk to him about his little fit he had. The only thing he could do was turn around and face her. Perhaps she would not even look at the monitor.

99% and holding.

He spun around on his swivel chair and looked at her. "What?"

The cold tone in his voice was unsettling.

"What indeed, Mr. Ward."

"I suggest you're inquiring about my so-called *jealousy*." He made quotations on the last word.

"I'm not sure what else would be the issue." Megan looked at him, expressionless.

"I'm not one to get jealous," Alister explained. "Concerned, yes."

"Concerned?"

"I don't like the way Ugros looks at her. Not that I'm suggesting that I would rather her look at me. I think he has genuine feelings for her."

"So, what if he does. He's keeping it in check, unlike you."

"What are you implying, Mrs. Conners? That I'm hoping to hook up with your daughter? She's a bit too young for me, I'm afraid."

"That never stopped you from flirting with Sarah," Megan stated.

Alister's smirk turned into a scowl. "I'm done talking about it."

Megan looked apprehensive to speak. She then thought about him creeping on her daughter and managed to push herself. "Just keep away from her."

"No concern here." Alister spun back to the computer monitor.

It was still at 99%. He mumbled inaudibly under his breath.

"You have more to say?"

"No. Just these computers causing me a headache like usual."

"They're the best way to remain undetected," Megan added.

"If your husband thinks that then I endorse him." Alister remained blank-faced as the percentage reached one hundred and completed.

CHAPTER TWELVE

Carving their path.

The conga line of jeeps drove down the now cemented path to the harbor. Canopies of trees were kept lengthy to have overhang but not long enough to touch the vehicles. It all added to the aesthetic. A jungle vacation on a tropical island. It was almost too good to pass up for some of them.

Eight all-terrain company automobiles approached the harbor master, creeping to a stop. Gerald waved four of them onto the ferry as he smiled warmly. He put on the friendly demeanor well considering he had just terminated two more local dockhands on account of superstition. They were short staffed but promised it would be made up to them when more funding came through.

As far as Gerald was concerned, Fracis could afford it. He was still trying to figure out how he could not afford it when the guests started getting out of the jeeps and walking around the ferry. He sighed inwardly. *At least the trip was only fifteen minutes one-way.*

"Whaaaa!"

A child, no more than six, began to scream. Gerald normally would not care but, seeing as how this was the first trip with actual guests, he took it as a sign for things to come. He let out a low groan.

"Hey, what gives?" one of them, presumably the whining kid's parent asked. "He's only a kid."

"No offence, mister. I'm just not used to hearing babies cry after having been out here for so long."

"Who're you calling a baby?" The boy instantly stopped waling and looked him directly in the eyes.

Geez, this is going to be a long fifteen minutes.

There was tension strung like a guitar string, so tight it was liable to snap. Everyone kept quiet except the boy who continued bellowing as if his toes were being stepped on. It went on like that for the whole trip. Eventually they arrived at the dock and were greeted by Sarah and Peter.

"I want to speak with the manager!" The adult who complained rushed up to them shortly after they docked.

"What seems to be the trouble, sir?"

"That boatman has no courtesy. He was very rude to us and should be fired."

"I'm sorry, Mr…"

"My name is Ferrand, Eugine Ferrand."

"Well, Mr. Ferrand, I'll have a word with our harbor master," Sarah said politely.

"Yeah. You do that." Eugine walked up to the top of the hill.

He glanced back over his shoulder and then spun around in shock. That woman was speaking with the boatman. Then it dawned on him. He must be the harbor master too.

"Shit," Eugine spat.

Harbor masters were always tricky to control. He did not like to work with them nor against them. Best not piss off the harbor master if you want to have a ride back.

Continuing up the hillside steps, his boy tugged on his suit cuff. "Daddy!"

Eugine was too busy looking back to really pay attention to the annoying little brat he called his son.

The first step onto the grass felt refreshing. Everyone had been standing for so long on the ferry and walking on cement that the soft comfort of the laid out, faux lawn was a welcome change.

Peter led the way as Sarah caught up to them, hanging back to answer any questions that may be asked from the back of the line.

"So what's featured in this park?" one of the guests, an elderly woman wearing fancy pearls around her neck, asked.

"Well, we have a wide variety of exhibits featuring the most fascinating animals," Sarah smiled. "There is also a food court with food prepared already. Most of the menu consists of tropical treats but there is a vegan menu as well."

"What kind of animals?" asked a man who was balding but still tried to maintain his long brown hair. He made up for the cranium catastrophe with a full beard.

"That's what we are hoping you will find most interesting," Sarah told him.

"It's got to be reptiles of sorts," the snot-nosed kid up front screamed.

"Don't you think the title is a bit confusing? People would have to look up what a saurian is in order to understand it fully," his father explained.

"No more confusing than any other scientific name really," Peter answered him. "Please. Right this way. We'll get you checked in, stop for a bite, go over the itinerary for the day, and then have the big reveal."

The group of twelve investors and one kid followed Peter into the main lobby where Francis stood with arms wide open.

"Welcome to Saurian Safari, everyone!"

***

Daisy stood before the mirror in her bungalow. When she had scrambled out of the sorority, she had only grabbed a few belongings and even fewer things to wear. She was happy she grabbed what she was dressed in now.

It was a light pink, satin gown and had a beaded strap that crisscrossed around her neck and connected to a middle piece on her chest that formed a heart. She smiled as she looked it over. The dress felt pleasant to the touch and fit snug around her trim frame.

There was a knock at her door.

She took one more look at herself and then strode across to the door. When she opened it, she saw her mother standing there.

"Woah! You look stunning!" Megan beamed.

"Thanks. I'm just glad I don't have to show Ugros today. Gives me a chance to throw this old thing on."

"It looks familiar."

"Yep. I wore it to prom."

"Ah, that's right!" Megan smiled. "Are you almost ready?"

Daisy brushed her hair away from the side of her face. "Um, yes. Let me just put my earrings on."

She dashed across the room in her pink high heels and put them on. They were in the shape of diamonds.

The two then rushed out of the room and towards the dining hall. As they rounded the corner, they saw Alister making his way towards their direction.

"What are you doing here?" Megan said suddenly.

"I came to talk with both of you." Alister smiled his usual creepy smile.

"This area is reserved for Daisy. There is no reason for you to be here."

"Like I said, I have something I need to talk about." Alister tried to remain calm. Inwardly, he did not feel like repeating himself.

"Well then, out with it."

Alister took a deep breath and looked from Megan to Daisy. "There have been rumors. Rumors about me trying to, for lack of a better word, *be* with you."

"Oh?" Daisy tried to act oblivious.

"Please. Don't act shocked. I know everyone thinks it."

"We're going." Megan grabbed Daisy around her arm and hurried around him.

"You look so beautiful today!" Alister blurted.

None of them knew if he meant to say it, not even the professor himself.

"I apologize."

Megan spun around on her heel and marched up to him. "You stay away from my daughter! If there are any further complaints, I'll have you fired."

He looked at Daisy who would not make eye contact. "As you wish."

The two then made their way down the hallway, leaving Alister with his thoughts.

***

Once everyone was checked in, most of them made their way directly to their rooms. Everyone except Eugine. He was standing over the wishing well looking at his reflection. Another appeared next to him. Francis' signature, wide, friendly smile spread across his face.

"How's it going, Ferrand?"

"Conners. I hope your exhibits are worth the trip out here. When I expected to be brought halfway across the world to see some attraction of yours, I thought the least you could do was pay for my ticket."

Francis laughed. Eugine did not.

"Listen, Ferrand. If you like what you see, I'll pay for your trip back. How's that sound?" He patted him on the back.

"Better than nothing. Hell, it better be worth it, Conners. Your expeditions were costly for Worldly Venturers. I would hate to see some random reptile exhibit with a rare snake or crocodile, or some shit kids could see on the Discovery Channel."

Francis patted him on the back again, slower this time. "Boy, are you going to be in for a surprise."

"Yeah, Speaking of boys, where's my snot-nosed little twerp? Milton! Milton get out here!"

The kid came running as if Eugine was his drill sergeant. “Whaaaaaat, Dad!”

“Don’t give me that. Where were you?”

“I was looking at the gift shop.”

“Well, wait until Mr. Conners here gives you the okay to go wandering off.”

Milton wanted to tell his dad what he actually saw. He knew it was too fantastic for a parent to believe. Especially his father. If he were a bit older, maybe. Maybe he would tell him of the large stegosaurus that was roaming the lawn. Or of the man who was guiding it somewhere.

***

About half an hour later, everyone joined up in the dining hall. Daisy and Megan sat on stage while Francis was standing behind the podium. The whole set up was temporary but not crude in construction. It would hold until it was taken apart.

Eugine and Milton were sat at a table near the front while the rest of the visitors were scattered around. Some were at the bar while one was trying to chat up Aly. She casually shrugged him off.

“Ladies and gentlemen. May I have your attention please!” Francis said into the microphone.

Most of the guests looked up. One at the bar barely even gave him the time of day while the one by Aly was trying continuously to get under her apron.

“It’s time. Please gather this way,” he announced with an authoritative yet friendly tone.

Some sighed while the rest listened right away. Francis smiled broadly and held up his hands. “Shall we begin?”

Between Megan and Daisy there was a projector screen. It was 6x10 and dangling a couple of feet off the ground. Enough for them all to see.

The lights dimmed and the screen lit up. It showed a picture of the jungle.

“The Congo. One of life’s great sanctuaries. Most of which has not been explored. We here at Saurian Safari have invested greatly in time and connections. As some of you know, these discoveries did not just show up. Locals were asked, expeditions were funded and prepared. What we have found will rock the world.” He paused for effect. “These reptiles are unlike anything any living man has ever seen. No one could have predicted what we'd find out there, nor how many. It was a true delight when we encountered our first specimen."

A press of a button brought about another slide. "This here is our first specimen we came across. It was not a reptile so would not fit with the park's theme. Nor was it anything compared to what we would eventually find. This animal here is a megapiranha. It was found washed up ashore along a river in the Congo. It measured a meter and a half in length. It was our first sign that something big was in our futures."

Another slide came up. "Here is a village, just on the outskirts of the Congo. It is where we heard of local legends of strange animals running around the jungle at night. They mostly stuck to the wood line but would occasionally be seen attacking small rodents. Eventually, villagers started going missing."

"Are you saying the animals in your park have taken human life?" one of the guests, a woman with a snooty look on her face, asked.

"Not quite. We cannot say for certain what these creatures have eaten. Much like you wouldn't be able to tell if a lion or tiger killed someone before being put in a zoo," Francis explained.

No one responded as the projector rose up into the ceiling.

"I think it's time we get this tour underway." Francis smiled again. "We've got a lot of ground to cover."

CHAPTER THIRTEEN

An evolutionary crossing.

The entrance to the titular safari was covered in faux leaves and shrubbery. The plastic pieces were crafted to look as realistic as possible. There was even moisture seeping out of them. Along the floor was a dirt path that was, in fact, a rug that stretched along the pathway. It looked like mud and even had big reptilian footprints imprinted in it. They spread three feet across.

Everyone was taken aback by how lifelike the exhibit was. The twelve visitors felt like they were in some kind of tropical environment. Yet the rooms contained a cool temperature that was a desirable seventy-two degrees. They had crossed the threshold of human intervention and were now stepping into some lost world.

Milton could not stop staring at the floor. "These tracks have a long distance between them."

Eugine nodded. "I agree with my son. Just how big are these reptiles?"

"All will be revealed shortly." Francis smiled.

His wife stood by his side as Daisy was behind them. The look of excitement covered their faces. For Francis and Megan, the wait had been excruciating. Years of preparation all depended on this event.

Two young men, brothers, kept ogling Daisy's rear. Their father, an older gentleman with a quick temper, noticed and nearly smacked them upside the head. He figured they needed discipline but now was not the time nor place.

"This is what we like to call the saurian sanctuary. On this safari, we will encounter rare animals that were thought long extinct," Francis explained.

"You mean like the frill shark?" Milton asked.

"Yes, in a way. We don't have any aquatic reptiles here… yet." Francis smiled at the boy.

"What do you have here then?" a woman asked.

This particular woman Francis had been trying to maintain eye contact with the whole day. She was the richest of them all but also the most hideous. Some had declared she was fifty going on eighty. He tried to mind his own business.

"We have a little walk to go. Until then, I suggest you absorb the atmosphere."

"The vibes this place is giving off remind me of Vietnam," the father of the two young men stated.

"Trust me, sir. There are no scares on this tour. Only wonders and amazement." Megan looked over her shoulder at him.

The man, beside himself, could not get over how angelic her features were. He realized he was staring at her just as his sons stared at her daughter. He shook his head slightly.

"The apple doesn't fall far from the tree, aye Paps?" one of his sons told him.

This time, he did get a much-deserved smack on the back of his head.

Peter and Sarah brought up the rear. They were on standby for both questions and instructions.

As they approached the first exhibit, Francis' palms began to get sweaty. He was growing nervous, and Megan could tell. She then stepped in.

"Here we are, at our first showcasing of a mighty saurian."

"Yes!" Francis beamed.

"Where are the plaques to tell us what it is?" the woman of unknown age inquired.

"For now, they are not set up. They will be once the park is open for business," Megan explained.

"What are those?" Milton pointed to the two holes under the large glass pane.

"They look like you can put your hands in them?" Eugine stated.

"You can fit most of your arm in there. They are there so tourists can feed it," Francis explained.

"Feed what?" one of the brothers asked.

Francis was already getting worried. There was no sign of the stegosaurus in its enclosure. "Here, I'll demonstrate."

As he walked over, Peter spoke into his walkie talkie. "Feeding time."

There was a response on the other end. Then came a mechanical noise that could be heard near the enclosure. Everyone looked down in time to see a pile of mashed up grass fill a metal tray, visible through the glass.

"Looks like the stuff Mom ate when she went on her Keto diet." The brothers laughed and gave each other a high-five.

Unbeknownst to them, it was filled with more than just grass and minerals but a healthy supply of vitamins. Francis slid both his arms into the slots and reached down. He successfully pulled up some of the slop.

"Now," Peter said calmly.

The low droning of an alarm could be heard. Francis waited eagerly. The alarm rang again and, still, nothing came.

"Are we supposed to be seeing something?" Eugine asked.

Minutes passed. Bored sighs and groans could be heard.

"He must not be hungry." Francis waited a little longer.

The lingering feeling of dread that overcame him was impossible to ignore. There was something wrong. He stuck his arms in further while simultaneously holding the grassy goop out as far as he could.

Nothing.

Some of them expected a pair of hideous jaws to come out and rip him right through the glass. When Francis pulled back, that appeared not to be the case.

"So much for act one," Eugine chuckled.

"There is plenty more to see. Come with me." Francis was annoyed but would not take it out on them.

They all continued on down through the faux jungle hallway.

***

Catt Brooke drove down the winding path that led to the harbor. By her side was her purse which held a tape recorder. She already had everything all set, all she had to do was hit the big red button. She felt nervous doing this job. There was a certain risk factor she was not comfortable with.

It went beyond her position as an investigative reporter. Human lives were at risk. Peter Denning's life was at risk. She had kicked herself for not looking into the Saurian Safari staff more.

She could not believe Alister Ward slipped through the cracks and became a part of the Conners' staff. He was what he claimed, a herpetologist who specialized in carnivores. Yet there was a whole other side to him.

Speeding towards the ferry, Gerald waved her down.

"Hey! This is a restricted area. I need to see credentials."

Without hesitating, she reached into her bag. What she pulled out was not papers or cards, but rather a small pistol. She pointed it right at him. He was taken aback.

"Don't do anything stupid, lady," Gerald pleaded.

"This is an emergency. I need to get to Darken Island. People are in trouble."

"Maybe I should call them first." Gerald began to reach for his phone. "You know, just to give them a heads up."

"Don't bother! I already tried," Catt stated.

"I was just talking to them half an hour ago."

"It'd only take a few minutes to cut off communications," Catt explained. "Look, just get the ferry ready. We need to get there pronto."

Two of Gerald's employees walked over. He turned to them and nodded. "Alright. Let's get this lady over there. She seems serious."

"I'm dead serious," she replied coldly.

"No, you're just dead." Gerald swiftly reached for his side piece.

Catt aimed and fired, blowing off a couple of Gerald's fingers on his right hand.

One of the workmen turned tail while the other charged for her.

Without wasting more ammo, she pushed down hard on the accelerator and barreled down onto the ferry. She then got out and went over to the console. It seemed simple enough to work so she started the ignition and pushed the throttle forward. She then steered away just as the workman who had run away returned with guns.

"Money talks, huh?" she yelled over her shoulder.

They were about to fire when Gerald shouted, "Don't!"

Quickly obeying the order, they lowered their machine guns.

"We just have to rethink our strategy."

"Let's rent out a chopper. I know a guy in the military who can hook us up," one of the African workmen said. "He's my brother-in-law."

"Then get him on the phone, now!" Gerald cursed as he clutched his hand.

Catt did not look back. She feared they had a gun trained on her, pointed at her head for absolute damage. She waited but the gunshot never came. Continuing forward, she began to worry. There was no way to get to Peter or the others in time. There was sabotage at play, probably by the time she found out there was even a problem.

Water rushed past the ferry as she pushed it to its full extent. She glanced down and saw the choppy waves brushing against the hull. There was no telling what she would discover at Darken Island. That island had been a place of death for so long.

Her friends had stories to tell about that place. None were good. She had come here from Massachusetts to broaden her view and opportunities. She liked Cape Town, but the local news was not cutting it. It was mostly drug and gang related.

She now had an inside scoop. One that her editor allowed her to run with. There was no telling what kind of promotion she would receive and yet she did not care. She had to warn them. One of Worldly Venture's most disgruntled employees had come to her last week.

The man had gone by the name of Bill, but she knew it was just a cover. He had slipped a file under her office door. When she saw it the following day, her mind began to run.

She managed to track 'Bill' down through the fingerprints he left on the envelope and a favor she had acquired from a friend in forensics. His real name was Regenold Feilding, and he was not just some employee. He was the former CEO of Worldly Ventures. He relayed the plan concocted by them and how he had wanted no part in it.

Now, there was only so much she could do. She just hoped she was not too late.

CHAPTER FOURTEEN

It was the experience.

Blending an event of such magnitude with such a lax presentation was something Francis was having trouble with, containing his genuine excitement. It had all built up to this. With Megan and Daisy by his side, he knew he had support beyond the investors that were walking behind them.

Soon, they came to the next exhibit. The Utahraptor triplets. Francis had made sure to study the young Milton to gage how far he could push the terrifying sight of these creepy critters. The boy was strong headed and spoiled but that did not mean he would not fear the eerie sight of them staring at him from the dark.

Francis brushed some of the faux leaves out of the way and held them aside so others could pass through. The room was dim, almost too dark to see to the other end.

Eugine could make out a long glass tank of sorts on the other side of the room. It was barely luminated by a red glow coming from the ceiling. The heater kept the enclosure warm, but outside was a cool seventy-two degrees.

The hellish sight was only amplified when demonic glowing eyes darted around at them.

"What are they?" The ugly old woman was repulsed.

"You'll all find out shortly. Needless to say, they're not pretty," Peter chuckled from the rear of the group.

"Daddy." Milton tugged at his father's suit jacket sleeve. He was clearly scared but too proud to admit it. The word held a weakness he was not willing to showcase.

"Can they see in the dark?" one of the brothers asked.

"We think so," Francis stated.

"We're ready to lighten the room," a voice over the intercom announced.

"Go for it." Francis smiled.

The room they were in began to brighten slowly.

At first, the investors did not know what to think. They looked like tall lizards that stood on their hind legs. No one could place them. Not in the current line-up of modern-day reptiles.

Then Milton spoke up. "Utahraptor?"

"Yes!" Francis cheered. "They are a species of theropod that lived a long time ago."

"What are you saying?" Eugine inquired. "Are these dinosaurs?"

Francis' face glowed with happiness. "Three of the thirteen we have here at Saurian Safari."

"You must be joking! Dinosaurs have feathers," one of the brothers laughed.

"Tell that to them," Daisy nodded towards the two creatures.

Snooty bitch. Both brothers thought simultaneously, unbeknownst to each other.

One of the Utahraptors turned around and made its way further into the enclosure.

"What's it doing?" Eugine asked.

"I think it's rendering," the father of the two brothers laughed.

"It's not of computer materials. These animals are flesh and blood." Francis wanted to shout but kept his tone level enough not to sound annoyed.

Slam.

The Utahraptor rammed into the glass, causing it to shutter. Even the guests felt it.

"Cool surround sound," the father continued.

"Believe what you want, Mr. Hayes. These creatures are the real deal."

"Prove it," he retorted.

"When we get more herbivores in here, you'll see. I'll even open a petting zoo for the infants."

"Why not now?"

"They're carnivores. They'll tear you apart," Daisy scoffed at him.

"Then get that stegosaurus back. I want to feed it," Hayes demanded.

"We'll take you to it personally after the tour. It's only a juvenile so it should not be too aggressive," Francis explained.

Megan looked to him, taken aback. "Franky, isn't that a bit risky?"

"I'm all about risks, Meg. Now please. Let's finish the tour."

The tour continued for a while. Everyone was growing slightly fatigued, but it was hard to tell if it was the actual terrain or the fancy attire everyone was wearing. Every guest looked like they had just walked out of a wardrobe for the Oscars. The only two that did not seem phased were Sarah and Peter but that had to do with their safari getup.

Francis turned back to the crowd. "Alright, everyone. We've shown you about half the dinosaurs in this park. We're now making our way to the second dining hall where there will be refreshments."

"Oh, thank God!" Mr. Hayes said.

His sons, Todd and Roy, groaned in agreement.

The older woman of unknown age, whom Francis kept forgetting her name was Ms. Kragle, sighed.

"Is something the matter?" Francis asked her.

"I was hoping for a grander exhibit."

Francis was taken aback. *My technicians and set decorators have worked for nearly two months on the design of the jungle setting. Now what, this hag queen's going to criticize it? On top of everything, what else could possibly go wrong?*

"What would you like to see in a future adaptation of a recreation of the Congo, Ms. Kragle?"

"Perhaps some more sounds. We've been walking around in stark silence this whole time."

Again, Francis was shocked. This time not so much directed at her but at himself. "I'm sorry. It's an oversight we'll get right on."

"I would hope so."

She may have been snooty, but she had a point, Francis thought as he led the group out of the artificial jungle and into the dining hall.

***

The stegosaurus was ushered over towards a nearby field. Alister did not have time to put it in a new containment. He did not want to raise any suspicion. He gave the juvenile herbivore a swift kick on one of its back legs and it groaned. It did not fight back but rather slowly lumbered to a large patch of grass and began to gorge on it.

"Stupid cow," Alister snarled and then turned back towards the facility.

He could see through the glass windows that Francis was seeing to his guests. Daisy was there, looking as fetching as ever in her light pink, satin gown. Megan sat next to her. Her daughter, the practical embodiment of her. The sight of them gave him some regret about what he was about to do.

Thinking over the plan, he quickly made his way towards the carnivore enclosures. Namely the Spinosaurus.

Slipping through the doors, he briskly walked down the hall and towards the exhibits. He saw no sign of anyone. His timing had been perfect. He just had to get the big dumb lizard out of there and lure it to where he wanted it to go. Coming to one of the doors labeled *authorized personnel only*, he slid his key card and entered. The door slid shut behind him.

***

Daisy was getting fed up with the party. It had only been ten minutes and already she felt like she needed fresh air. The Hayes brothers kept ogling her, staring at her buxom chest. She did not think she was above them. Rather, they seemed like chauvinistic pigs. She tried to focus on her margarita, but it was beginning to get annoying. Their egregious fawning was pitiful.

She slowly stood up and placed her napkin on the table. “I’m going to check on Ugros.”

Megan turned to her. The table was reserved for them and there were no other prying eyes or eavesdroppers around. “I’m sure he’s fine.”

“I must be sure. It’s not just a big day for me. He needs to know.”

“Do you think he’ll understand?”

“I think he will.” She gave a faint smile and then hurried down the hall. A couple of whistles accompanied her exit.

Before she knew it, she was walking through the dim jungle set alone. It was rather eerie. There were no sounds. It was an odd silence, like there needed to be noise. She held her hands close to her chest. Faux leaves brushed against her. They were moist, water added to them for that extra touch of realism. She passed through and found herself in the rest of the carnivore hall. It was cold and uninviting.

There was no one there either.

All the way to the other end was a set of big bulky doors. She hurried as fast as her diamond-crested high heels could take her. There were low grumbles that could be heard over the speakers. She knew they were the real thing. She passed by the tyrannosaur exhibit and nearly froze.

There they were. The three of them. Mother, father, and child, standing by the glass. It was as if they were waiting for someone to open their enclosure to let them out. She was now in a panic. She sped towards the doors and swung them open. She was safe.

The observation room was empty. Jason was not there nor were Stanton or Grover. She walked through and realized the computers were on, but they were not registering anything. There was technobabble and code written all across the screen, but it really did not mean anything to her. She slowly walked over towards the door that led to the enclosure and typed on the keypad. It opened with a whooshing sound. Before her was the greenery and foliage that she had grown accustomed to these past months.

Ugros was sitting over by the swampy water, looking down at it. At first, she thought he was looking for trout which had been stocked there earlier that week. After a few minutes, she realized he was looking at his reflection. She began to wonder if he loathed himself for his appearance. A sense of sadness swept over her. She vowed then and there that she would have her father try to fix him to look normal. To be normal.

She took one step down the metal staircase, her high heel making a clopping sound. Ugros looked up at her and smiled. He seemed transfixed by her expression. To him, she seemed sad, like something was wrong, and did not end well. Soon, she was walking on the grass. She shook her high heels off and walked over to him. He stood up, making a grunting sound as if his joints ached. Closing the distance, she suddenly realized just how naked he was. He was completely exposed, his manhood pulsating at the very sight of her nearness. She quickly held out her hand for him to take and ushered him over towards the trees.

***

The boat brushed against the shoreline; the sand could be heard crunching under the hull. It slid onto the beach where Catt quickly got off. She secured the rope to a nearby large chunk of driftwood and then made her way towards the pathway.

As far as she could tell, there was no one on the beach. No one saw her sneak ashore. She figured they would have detained her on sight given that the harbor master had probably already blown the whistle. Instead, she was alone in the jungle. The sounds of hollering monkeys and exotic birds chirping filled the area. She was surrounded by life yet felt so alone.

A light wind blew through the canopy overhead. It brought with it a whistling sound that made her shiver. She felt so uncomfortable. She was not sure how far these men were willing to go but she knew, to them, she was expendable.

Eventually arriving by a fenced off portion of the area, she grabbed a stick and tested it for an electrical current. She received no shock, no sparks, nothing. Deep down she wished she had a pair of bolt cutters or something to create a hole. Instead, she stuck her foot in one of the gaps and hoisted herself up with her hands. As she repeated the process, the feeling of isolation became more and more abundant. It was not that she was alone on the island. It was that she had no one to help her out here. She doubted she could get anyone on the staff to listen to her, but she had to try. For the sake of them all.

***

"This is such a drag." Todd Hayes turned to his brother and sighed.

Roy took a deep breath while scanning the area. Ever since the buxom brunette with the pink dress disappeared, things had gone down the toilet. All the social mingling and obnoxious laughter was driving him crazy.

"Let's go exploring," Todd whispered to him.

"How do we even go about leaving without supervision?"

"We get up to go to the Jane's Juice Jamboree. That place is the closest to the exit. Then, we can make our escape," Todd suggested.

Roy liked the idea but wished it was not that joint. The woman there was almost as pretty as Conners' daughter. He did not want to make it seem like he was interested and then run off. He looked around for another restaurant or concession area but realized Todd was right. It was their best bet.

"Dad. We're going to go get some drinks. We'll be right back." Roy turned to their father.

"Get me something sweet please," Mr. Hayes responded.

Both young men shot up and hurried over to the refreshment area. Roy noticed the woman was serving that Ms. Kragle lady who looked dissatisfied with her order. She was not even looking in their direction, much less paying attention to them. It was now or never. Todd was the first to hurry around the establishment. Roy quickly followed and they soon found themselves entering the hallway in mere seconds.

CHAPTER FIFTEEN

He was different.

Daisy Conners expected the hulking brute to be rough and unmerciful. As she lay atop Ugros, looking up into the artificial tropical canopy, she felt the world was open to her. His rhythmic breathing caused his chest to rise and fall so aggressively that she was given the impression she was sitting atop one of those gym balls but constantly deflating and reinflating. The feeling of his leathery hide against her soft skin was such a contrast but neither minded.

Ugros had felt the urge for months while Daisy seemed to be just coming around to the idea. He had not expected to see her today, looking as beautiful as she did. He understood what she wanted based on the gentle aura of her teachings. He carefully lifted a hand the size of a catcher's mitt and began to stroke her light brown hair. She moaned to his touch.

Then Daisy swung her leg over his girthy stomach. She looked at him, giving him appraisal with her eyes. "I think it's time we caught you up on modern times."

She felt down and grabbed his manhood, gently stroking it to make him erect. It took a moment to find the tip but, when she did, she did not hesitate to bring it closer to her own privates. He was grinning now as she slid the slimy appendage into her further and further. She gasped several times before she began to move, the rhythmic surge was like a shock to her system.

***

"It's here!" Todd called his brother over.

"Keep quiet, you imbecile!" Roy hushed him as he approached. "I don't want to get caught snooping!"

Todd laughed. "It's not like we're doing anything illegal!"

"I guess not. Let's just get this over with, quick."

Roy looked inside the exhibit. It was rather dim but there was clearly a thin haze hovering over the ground. The leaves were bright green. He then turned and saw Todd wasting no time sticking his hands in the contraption under the window.

"This is ridiculous," Roy stated. "Dad said they were just holograms."

"Then there's nothing to fear," Todd said.

There was a sharp whooshing sound as a tray full of leaves flung out under the electronic arms. Todd reached inside and managed to get a grip on a few of them. He then extended his reach out. They were separated by several inches of wall and a thick pane of glass. Roy still felt uneasy.

Waiting, watching, a snapping sound could be heard. Something was coming. Something big. Roy was practically pressing his face against the glass. The breaking of branches and rustling of leaves were growing in intensity.

"What dinosaur was in this exhibit again?" Roy turned to Todd, asking.

"Stegosaurus." Todd looked away for a moment. "Don't worry. They're large in size. As big as carnivores."

"But didn't Francis say it was a juvenile?" Roy looked at his brother.

A low growl could be heard and the two looked back slowly in unison.

"Is that a stegosaurus?"

"I don't know," Todd said. "I know they have big things sticking out of their backs. It's got to be."

The bipedal animal stood twenty feet off the ground. It marched over towards the viewing window and scanned it.

"Do you think it can see us?" Roy asked nervously.

Before he could answer, the massive creature leaned forward and sniffed the robotic hands.

"Dude, pull out," Roy ordered.

"I think it's going to take them." Todd raised his hands up higher.

They watched as it studied them. Its upper lip curled.

"You cannot be serious!" Roy was stepping back now.

"I think this place is going to make Dad a for-."

The long crocodile-like jaws opened and suddenly closed down hard on the robotic arms.

"Jesus! Pull out!" Roy cried.

"I can't!" Todd screamed, panicking. "They're stuck."

Roy hurried over and began to tug Todd around his waist. They both looked at the animal which was staring into their eyes as if eating into their souls.

"Get me out of here!" Todd shrieked.

There was another tug and they both fell to the ground. Todd recovered quickly and looked down. His right arm was badly mutilated while his left one was gone. Blood squirted out from the stump. Roy had never heard his brother scream the way he did.

He quickly stood up and grabbed Todd under his armpits and began to drag him away.

The carnivore let out a terrible roar which echoed over the speakers. Roy fought the urge to cover his ears.

Bang.

Roy and Todd quickly looked up and saw that the dinosaur was now slamming its cranium into the glass. It was not long before cracks began to spread out. It looked like a large spider web spun by the world's fastest spider.

"Go!" Todd told his brother.

"I'm not leaving you." Tears formed in Roy's eyes.

"Get out of here." His voice was growing weak as blood continuously pumped out of his wounds.

In less than ten seconds, the glass shattered. Roy had just rounded the corner when the sound of smashing glass made him drop his brother in fear. He went to pick him up but Todd grabbed his arm and bit it.

"Ow! What are you doing?"

"Get out of here! We'll both die if you stay."

Roy could not find it in himself to leave his only brother behind. Their childhood flashed before his eyes. Memories of building sandcastles on the beach, his brother digging a huge hole to sit in. Tears began to fill his eyes.

"Go!" Todd screamed. "Don't start crying. If you don't make it, I'll hate myself forever."

He did not argue. Instead, he leaned forward and kissed his brother's head. He already felt cold. Roy then got up and ran further into the building. He was going for the exit. The restaurant was on the other side of the building. There were only so many options.

The screams of his brother being devoured caused him to start sobbing while running.

The Spinosaurus had never felt so nourished. Its appetite was not satiated but the gratifying taste of the morsel caused it to crave more. After swallowing the body in parts, the blood flowed like juice down its gullet. It was akin to the taste of fish and some lizards it had eaten in the Congo. Though the prey was easier to obtain and it did taste better, there was a faint sensation, like numbing on its tongue. The plasma poured out like a juicy waterfall. The floor beneath it was covered in red as opposed to the off white of its normal shade.

Turning its head to the left, it sensed the other prey had run in that direction. A faint, muffled roar off to its right drew its attention and it stormed after it. There was familiarity in the tone. An ancient rival.

***

Alister Ward was situated in a small section of the control room. His laptop rested on his knees as he leaned forward and fidgeted with a few switches. To the untrained eye, it looked like he was playing with them as if they were merely buttons to impress a toddler. They all glowed in various reds and blues. He reached forward and found the sole yellow button.

"No going back now." He licked his thin lips and pressed it.

***

She felt she was bouncing on clouds. Despite the unspecified difference in centuries, the gap longer than any living couple's, she felt at one with Ugros. He had been so tender during the entire act up to this point. She could tell he was almost done by the more violent thrusting.

Giving one loud moan, she began to climb off. She did not want to be finished but he had done well. There were other tricks she could teach him, especially with his abnormally long tongue. She pushed him off, ready to dismantle the beast, when the lights went out.

Collapsing atop him, she was immediately plunged into blackness. It was the suddenness that startled her the most.

"Raaaaggh," Ugros groaned.

A warm liquid pumped into her. She gasped suddenly.

"Oh no," she said, gravely.

***

"What the hell's going on?" Francis shouted.

Immediately, Peter and Sarah snapped into action. They began to assess the situation in their heads. If the power was out, the dinosaurs should still be in their exhibits. They just needed to get to the control room and figure out what had happened.

Francis began to panic. This was his first grand reveal for Saurian Safari. There was not room for error. He looked around. The light from the windows was the only source of visibility.

"Alright, everyone. Let's make our way towards the windows until we can get the power back on."

"Where are my boys?" Mr. Hayes shouted.

There was no response.

"They went to get me a drink. They haven't returned!"

"Great," Francis mumbled under his breath.

If either one of them had anything to do with the power going out, he would press charges. There was no doubt in his mind.

Peter managed to make his way over to Francis. "We need to get to the control room. Sarah will stay here and maintain the crowd."

Francis looked around for Megan. She was over by the windows trying to calm some of the staff. By her was Jason. He seemed to be handling himself with the barrage of questions well.

"Alright. Let's go," Francis said as he led the way out of the dining area.

***

The last thing Alister wanted was to have any witnesses. He looked over a display of options on a control board. They were labeled with each of the dinosaur's names. Things were going to wrap up and not neatly. He only wished he could have stuck around to witness the bloodshed.

With the flick of a switch, he put in a card he had acquired from the dead security guard around the corner and punched in the keys. It paid to have a supply of horse tranquilizers on hand.

The glass covers that were over each button suddenly sprung open. Alister smiled widely as he began to press each one.

"It's time for a real safari," he chuckled.

CHAPTER SIXTEEN

It worked too well.

Each cage opened with a slight creaking sound. Most of the dinosaurs did not even notice. It was a subtle noise that was mostly covered by the wall of artificial jungle noise. The Utahraptor enclosure was the first to see the exodus. All three carnivores saw the sliver of light peer in through the crack and were drawn to it. They sped out of the room, their long strides taking them faster than any big cat of the African variety.

Their nostrils were filled with strange new odors. They had grown accustomed to their own exhibit. As they branched out, they were boldly testing the area for any signs of easy prey. There were no immediate sights to consume. A strange electronic hiss did irritate them. They perceived it as a threat and charged the source.

Before they could find it, a massive clashing sound could be heard. There was something wrestling with its exhibit door. The three predators formed a U-shape around it and waited. It was not long before a round head stuck out from behind its barrier. The long sails on its back were restraining it from fully fitting through the door.

The great Dimetrodon let out an angered growl towards the onlookers. They stared at it with hungry eyes. One of them took a few steps closer. They both snapped at each other. The Dimetrodon then backed into its enclosure.

As the door began to shut, three elongated claws wrapped around it. With a pull, the door swung open, and they entered its domain. Without hesitation, the Dimetrodon back crawled on its four short legs all the way towards the swampy, manmade lagoon.

One of the Utahraptors made a lunge for the creature. It managed to leap into the air and land next to it. Then, with a quick snap of its jaws, needle-like teeth sank into the scaly flesh. The Dimetrodon roared in pain and then snapped its head back. It chomped down on air as the Utahraptor quickly let go and backed away, hissing at its opponent.

Seeing the wide-open gap, the closest Utahraptor took its chance and swiftly charged at the fellow carnivore. When it was close enough, it lifted its foot high. Just as the Dimetrodon turned back, its claws dug into its soft head. Then, it used its toe muscles to dig its scythe claw into its skull. It dragged in a downward motion, exposing layers of flesh and muscle as the top of the Dimetrodon's face came apart.

The Utahraptor then extracted its claw as the others began to dig into its flesh. They struggled to get into the belly at first. Soon they managed to flip it over and relish in the innards.

Their delight did not last long. The strange hissing noise irritated them to no end now. After consuming enough intestines to qualify their kill as a bounty, they marched out of the exhibit and continued down the hallway.

***

Alister Ward never felt more in control. His whole life seemed to be observed under a microscope by some omniscient being. One that would stop his progress every time he tried to climb higher than his meager self. He now realized just how close he was to making himself a name to be feared.

Women would flock to him like a herd of Gallimimus galloping in a field. He could see it, the end of the world at the push of a button. He would expose the dinosaurs to the public and then mount an expedition to the Congo to drive them further towards populated areas. Investors would be begging him to have a part in weaponizing these creatures.

His ulterior motive was his alone. He knew how and when to push that metaphorical button. To have it all. He just had to put the lock on the system and then get off the island.

A swooshing sound could be heard. The door opened. No doubt they came to investigate why the power was out. He typed in a few keys and there was a clicking noise. The computer room was now locked.

Francis and Peter hurried through the control room. The hardware section was not far inside. Red lights spun atop the ceiling in the dark space. Both men slowed their pace as visibility became limited. Peter squinted, peering into the blackness.

Bumping into a table, Francis heard something tip and roll across it. It was coming for him. He reached out and grabbed to catch it. Feeling it in his grasp, he realized it was a flashlight. He fumbled for the button. With one click, the beam shone through the room.

Something was there. It took a moment for Francis' eyes to adjust. When they did, he saw it was his own reflection. He was standing in front of the window in the computer room. "Over here!" Peter turned and saw Francis making his way closer to the other side of the room. The door handle was on the right side of the closed off area.

"Ah, here it is." Francis reached down for the doorknob.

A guttural growl could be heard further off to his right. Francis took a deep breath and turned the light in that direction.

It lashed out at him with its clawed hand. The hot searing pain that shot through his chest made him gasp in surprise.

"Mr. Conners!" Peter shouted.

The flashlight fell from his boss' grip and onto the tile floor below. It spun around in a circle several times before landing on him. From what Peter could make out, the dinosaur was one of the Utahraptors. It was stepping on Francis' chest now, the scythe claw pressing into his skin.

"Help me!" Francis cried out.

Peter quickly felt around his person. He checked his pockets but nothing worth fighting a dinosaur was in them. He reached on his hip and produced a Bowie knife, unsheathing it with the grace of a Japanese samurai producing a custom sword. He was ready for battle.

"Hey!" he roared at the saurian.

It looked up at him and snarled. The claw did not stop its descent into his employer's chest. Peter took a few steps forward and was suddenly on the ground. He quickly looked up and saw a second Utahraptor standing over him.

"Sly bitch!"

The dinosaur shot forward, jaws open wide. Peter did the same with his blade and embedded it in its shoulder. He was aiming for the neck but the creature was too fast to calculate a direct hit. Still, it stumbled back, taking the weapon with it.

Francis began to gargle. Blood erupted from his mouth as he choked on it. The Utahraptor was sliding further down his stomach cavity.

"No!" Peter shouted.

There was no hope now. He could not grab the flashlight or his knife. All he could do now was turn and retreat. He reluctantly did so. He made it five feet when his stomach ran into a table corner. The wind was knocked out of him. He nearly collapsed but managed to grab onto one of the swivel chairs.

A screeching sound could be heard.

Peter turned and saw the third Utahraptor entering the room through the doorway.

"Unbelievable," he whispered hoarsely.

It wasted no time in charging at him. Peter felt helpless at that moment. He instinctively shoved the chair in its direction, but it was in the creature's favor. It hopped up with one foot and then used it to gain leverage, effectively pushing off the seat and soaring through the air at him.

The light suddenly began to spin in the room just as Peter ducked and rolled. He managed to quickly look over his shoulder. Francis was barely alive. The first Utahraptor was feasting on his insides. His hand was resting next to the flashlight.

Peter wanted to help him, but the man was clearly dead now. His last heroic act bought him precious seconds. He sprinted for the exit. He did not think he hit anything. He would deal with it if that obstacle arose.

Even though the flashlight had stopped spinning, the red warning lights were still causing him to feel a bit disorientated. He shook his head a few times to shake the dizziness. Soon, he realized he was already outside the room. He hurried down the hallway and towards the food court. He just hoped he was not too late.

Alister watched the cameras from inside the control room. He was impressed with what had just transpired. There was hope that Francis would be alive long enough to see the destruction of his park. It was not the end of the world for him. He still got to watch the carnivores rip and tear through his body like a pack of lions on a dead animal carcass.

He was fascinated that they acted like lions as well. The one with the blade in the chest was given plenty of shoulder room to get into the meal and have its fair share. They were indeed sharing but saving the easiest access points for the weaker of their pack.

The fact that the blade was still embedded in its chest made him wonder just how smart they were. They could not possibly know that if it were removed then it would bleed out. Perhaps the Congo had medicinal remedies for injuries such as this. Or the villagers knew more than what they were letting on. Maybe they taught these reptiles how to use the jungle as a natural healing device.

"Maybe I am going crazy after all," Alister chuckled.

CHAPTER SEVENTEEN

There she stood.

Intimidated by the awesome sight of the structure in front of her, Catt Brooke suddenly felt unsure. There was no guarantee that anyone would listen to her. The idea of her being escorted out immediately also came to mind. Though, when the lights went out, she began to worry that she was already too late.

There was no resistance or guarding at the doors to the dining hall. She was in a courtyard with small plants and wooden chairs. It all felt quaint. She knew it was deceiving. There was no doubt something was going wrong and people were going to be hurt, at the very least.

The doors were unlocked, and she had no problem opening them. There was the trepidation preceding the act. She took a deep breath and forced them open.

Inside there was a cacophony of shouting and screaming. They were all angry and concerned. Catt made her way along the windows and found a familiar face.

"Megan!" she called out for her.

She was busy trying to calm some of the guests but managed to catch Catt's voice among the crowd.

"Please, excuse me," Megan excused herself to an old hag in too much make up and then made her way over. "How did you get here?"

"There's no time to explain that! We're all in danger and need to get off this island."

"Francis and Peter should have the power back on any minute," Megan told her.

Catt felt uneasy at the idea of Peter being away from the group. "You don't understand. There's been a mutiny amongst your staff. He intends to…"

"Hey look!" a little boy shouted as he pointed out into the courtyard.

"What is it, Milton?" Eugine asked.

"Out there! In the lawn. Isn't that Roy?"

Some of the crowd stopped and looked towards where Milton was pointing. Sure enough, Roy Hayes was out there running across the grass. It was an odd sight. He looked like he had seen the devil.

Then there was a sudden thudding sound. Catt and Megan simultaneously noticed that a bowl of soup on a nearby table was beginning to show signs of ripples.

"Is that an earthquake?" a random man asked.

"I don't think so," Catt said gravely.

A large reptilian creature suddenly came into view. It was huge, standing over twenty feet tall at the very least. Everyone could see it now. A true dinosaur. They could also hear Roy screaming.

Mr. Hayes saw his son in such a fear the boy had never experienced before. It was only natural given his predicament. "I have to get out there!"

He began to make his way for the doors when Jason stopped him. "It's too late."

"The hell it is!" He shoved him out of the way.

"Oh my god!" Ms. Kragle shouted.

It was followed by several more gasps and screams. Mr. Hayes did not want to see what had just happened but felt obligated. There was an inkling that he would not like what he saw but he held out for hope that the dinosaur had narrowly missed him.

That was not the case. Roy was held in the predator's long, crocodilian jaws. It shook him back and forth. At first, he fought back but, eventually, he became limp. Blood began to pour onto the bright green grass below. It stained the creature's lower jaw and spilled down its chin like scarlet strands.

"No!" Mr. Hayes screamed in defiance.

It then flung him to the ground and wasted no time digging into his corpse. Innards were extracted as it forcefully tore them from his belly.

Some of the guests fainted, others turned and ran. Sarah was in shock. The creature she feared most was now running free and killing people. She felt lost.

Mr. Hayes was at a loss. He watched the predator tear apart his son. The only thing that crossed his mind was now there was no denying these prehistoric creatures were real and incredibly dangerous.

***

Something was off. At first, Grover and Stanton could not see in the dark room with the red flashing light. As their eyes adjusted to the flickering, they looked around the laboratory. Everything was off but nothing was out of place. It looked like it did during every shift. It was abnormally warm though.

Stanton noticed it first. "Shit!"

"What?" Grover asked.

"The door to Ugros' enclosure. It's not locked."

Grover walked up and realized it was true. Not only that, but the door was also cracked open.

"No wonder it's so hot in here." He pulled his lab coat off.

"We're going to have to check inside there," Stanton stated.

"I think we ought to call Jason first." Grover turned to face his colleague. "Better to be safe than..."

He paused.

"What?" Stanton asked.

"Sorry," Grover whispered fearfully.

A guttural hooting could be heard by the doorway to the laboratory. Stanton immediately froze in place. He could not move in fear that whatever was behind him would attack. The only muscle he moved was his mouth. "What's behind me?"

"Don't worry about that. Just stay still," Grover told the man.

Neither man was well versed in the multitude of dinosaurs in the exhibits. Grover was worried it was one of the Utahraptors but could not be sure. He observed it, taking in the sight of the six-foot-tall monstrosity. It had a crest atop its head. He tried to recall which dinosaurs had that. He knew the Spinosaurus and Dimetrodon had sails on their backs. There was nothing along this dinosaur's spine though. It could not be one of the Pteranodons. If so, where were its wings?

The creature began to arch its head back. The action was peculiar, and Grover thought it was about to lunge forward and bite Stanton's head off. Then, he realized.

"It's a Dilophosaurus!"

Splat.

The venomous saliva hit Grover in the face and in his eyes. He screamed wildly and accidently tripped over himself and onto the floor. Instinctively, Stanton ran to help his fallen friend. Sharp pain erupted on either side of his head. He then felt himself lifted off the ground as Grover cried.

Stanton screamed as blood trickled down his cheeks. There was a crunching sound, and he felt his skull cave in just as his head left his body.

“Help me!” Grover felt around.

It did not matter if the lights were off or not now. He was in a world of permanent darkness. Blinded by the dinosaur’s saliva, the fact slowly dawned on him. He panicked and got up. He could hear the carnivore ripping into Stanton as well as a second screech as the second Dilophosaurus entered the room.

“No!” He ran in the direction of the door, nearly tripping over a chair.

“What’s going on in there?” Daisy said while hiding behind Ugros.

The lights suddenly came on in the exhibit. The control room was still dark though. Daisy began to wonder if someone was controlling the power for Saurian Safari. She did not get time to think too long about it as Grover came charging out of the laboratory and stumbled down the stairs. He had a black substance that was covering his face.

She began to make her way over to him while Ugros followed. His loud footsteps sent fear through Grover’s mind like a mental shock.

“Get away! Don’t kill me!”

“Grover! It’s okay. We’re-”

Daisy stopped mid-sentence when a horrible creature began to make its way into the exhibit. It walked down the stairs slowly and methodically as it watched her and Grover’s every move. She began to back away.

It let out a low hooting noise. Grover froze in place but the creature’s vision was not based on movement. It saw him and approached.

Grover sobbed as it leaned forward, examining his body. It then parted its jaws and quickly bit into the back of his neck.

“No!” Daisy cried out.

It lifted him into the air and swayed back and forth before shaking violently and snapping his neck. It then loosened its grip and Grover was sent flying into the nearby manmade swampy pool. Then, the Dilophosaurus focused its attention on Daisy. It wasted no time arching its head back and letting loose a stream of vile saliva.

Daisy squeezed her eyes shut, expecting it to hit her at any moment. It did not. She opened them and saw that Ugros’ arm was in front of her face. He then stood in front of her, shook the gunk off his forearm and charged for the creature.

It reared back again, ready to expel more venom from its jaws. Aiming was an impeccable attribute of the Dilophosaurus but timing the projectile was something else entirely. It had only brought its head forward halfway when it felt the rough fingers tightly grip around its exposed throat.

Ugros lifted the carnivore into the air by its neck and gave it a tight squeeze. It drooled the substance from its mouth before it began choking on its own blood. Ugros gathered some of the venomous substance and smeared it in the dinosaur's own eyes. The Dilophosaurus was then discarded and thrown into the same pool as Grover.

"Look out!" Daisy cried.

Her scream made him look back at her. He was not sure what she was saying entirely but he could tell from her tone that it was a warning. He felt something sticky hit the back of his neck. Reaching, he found a similar substance that the previous dinosaur had expelled from its orifice. It was inky black. He then looked up and saw a similar creature to the one he had just killed standing on the landing that led to the stairs. It too was rearing back, almost arching its head. Ugros raised his arm over his eyes in preparation. He was too far to catch it mid spit.

A shot suddenly rang out. Blood erupted from the front of the Dilophosaurus' neck. It made a gurgling hooting sound and began to feel around at its throat. It was like it was searching for the thing that was blocking its airflow. Its claws dug through its skin. Blood gushed, spilling down its chest before it collapsed onto the ground in a pool of its own crimson plasma.

Ugros lowered his arm and saw a familiar face. It was the man who had rescued him from the frozen cave.

"Jason!" Daisy shouted in relief.

"I don't want to know what's going on or why you're in here. I do, however, want to get to the bottom of the power situation."

Daisy looked slightly embarrassed which was not how Jason had expected her to look. She seemed to be more distraught about being caught and not the fact that she had just hooked up with a reptilian-neanderthal hybrid.

"Let's get out of here," Jason said.

"What about the light?" Daisy asked.

"I have a flashlight." He placed a hand on his hip where one was tucked into his beltloop.

"No, I mean why is there only power in here, but the laboratory is out?"

Jason thought for a moment. "Let's get to the control room. Your father and Peter are there. Maybe we can help."

Daisy was about to follow but stopped. “What about Ugros?”

“What about him?” Jason asked, a bit annoyed that she seemed more interested in him than the current situation.

“We can’t leave him here.”

“Yes. We can.”

“He killed one of the Dilophosauruses no problem. If we run into any more dinosaurs, I’m assuming you would want him out there with us.”

He chuckled. “I took one down too with a rifle. He stays here.”

“Well then I’m staying too.”

“What?”

“I don’t want to argue about it, Jason. He saved my life.”

There was a pause.

“Gah! Damnit. Give me a minute.” Jason scratched his short black hair. “If he comes and everything checks out and is alright, then he’s coming straight back in here. Either way, I’m going to have a talk with your father about your involvement with him.”

“What?” Daisy was visibly hurt. She looked like she had just been told her dog was going to have to be put down.

“We don’t have time for this.” Jason came down the stairs and approached Ugros. “You stay with us.”

As the man spoke slowly, Ugros picked up what he was implying. He gave a look that said he understood. It was the same one Jason saw when he first moved Ugros out of their enclosure in Beijing.

“Alright. Let’s go.”

CHAPTER EIGHTEEN

It was not going well.

Terrance Ferrand had been given two extensive surgeries since the initial operation. His leg was gone but he was not responding well to the medicine given to him. He would be lucid one day and catatonic the next. There was an occasion when he was almost comatose, but the doctors managed to bring him around.

The whole situation nearly gave Golmer a panic attack. Bruce was there to talk him down before he decided to rage out at the entire hospital staff. Now the two sat in the waiting room again. It had been some weeks of nonstop issues. Both were getting tired. Sick and fed up with all the false hope.

Bruce was over by the water cooler when he heard a buzzing noise. He quickly realized it was his phone that he had left on the table next to a sleeping Golmer. The man had barely slept and was looking worse for wear. His brother's life could end at any moment. He wanted to make sure to be there during his last breaths.

He went to answer it and saw that it was a name he did not expect to ever see. It was that journalist woman, Catt Brooke. He figured she was in some kind of jam and needed a quick story.

"Fucking reporters." Bruce answered the device. "This better be important."

"I need your help," Catt sounded panicked.

"I figured that's why you were calling."

She did not miss a beat. *"Listen! A lot of people are in danger here. I need an evac helicopter out here pronto."*

"People? Danger? Where?" Bruce wondered.

"I'm at Saurian Safari. There's been a mutiny. People are dying," Cat said in a pleading tone. "Please help us."

"Why should we? One of my guys is not doing well. His brother won't help if he's able to be here. I won't either."

"Please! You're the only option!"

"Call the coastguard!"

"You're closer. There isn't time to argue!" Catt was screaming now. *"At least two people are dead and I'm afraid more will follow. I think there's a bunch of guys coming to the island to clean up and not the dinosaurs. Us!"*

Bruce looked down at Golmer who was stirring. "I think helping you people has caused *us* enough damage."

"Tens of people will die who don't deserve it!"

"I've seen more die in a couple hours. The world's not a fair place, sweetheart. I'm sorry but we're grieving here."

"Do it for Peter!"

"Fuck Peter." Bruce hung up angrily.

"What's going on?" Golmer asked half-awake.

"Nothing, bud. Just a job."

"What job?"

"Peter needs our help yet again."

"Why?"

"It's not important."

Golmer was about to push when a grave-faced doctor came through the door.

"How's Terrance?" Bruce asked.

"You both should see him now. The infection is too severe. We can't stop it from reaching his heart I'm afraid."

"What?" Bruce nearly fell back.

"No!" Golmer, already sitting, had to grip the handle on the chair he was in for support.

Both men looked down at the floor as if it held answers to their burning questions.

"How long?" Bruce asked.

"We're estimating about three more hours."

"Let's go see him." Golmer stood up weakly.

The men followed the doctor through the doors. The sense that they would be seeing Terrance for the last time did not sit well with them. It hurt even more when they entered his room.

"Hey guys!" Terrance spoke with an enthusiasm that shocked them.

"I haven't told him yet," the doctor said.

"Why the hell not?" Bruce asked.

"Tell me what?" Terrance wondered.

"The medicine we gave him not only subdued the amount of pain but boosted his energy levels."

"What did you give him?"

"A serum he had signed off on," the doctor continued. "We had a psychologist come in and confirm that he was of sound mind when he accepted the drug."

"What drug?" Bruce asked, annoyedly.

"I don't have a name as of yet. In Layman's Terms, it's an antivenom to treat Komodo dragon saliva infection. Amoxicillin and Clavulanic acid mixed with Modafinil. It's to help stop it and keep the victim conscious."

"This antivenom. It didn't help?" Golmer asked sullenly.

"I'm afraid it's only temporary. We cannot predict what will happen in the next few hours."

"Am I going to die?" Terrance asked.

No one said a word.

He began to chuckle. Then laugh. "That's just wonderful. I wanted to die from an infection. Truly I did."

"There's no time for hysterics," the doctor said. "You need to say your goodbyes."

Golmer and Bruce did not even acknowledge the doctor. Not even as he left the room. Instead, they walked up and sat on opposite ends of the bed.

"Look at you. You can barely fit in the bed," Bruce sniggered.

"I may be a tall bastard but at least I don't have your scar." Terrance pointed at the man's face.

"Hey, chicks dig scars."

"Speaking of chicks. How's Ms. Brook doing?"

"The reporter?" Golmer asked.

"Yeah. She was real pretty."

"Well, I'll make sure to tell her you said that," Golmer said reasurringly.

"I want to tell her." Terrance's smile widened. "Let me see your phone, Bruce."

Bruce did not budge.

"What's the matter? You saved her number, right? Please tell me you did!"

"I have it."

"Then what's the deal? Let me call her. I'm dying, aren't I?"

"Yes."

"I knew it!" Terrance reached for the phone that was sticking halfway out his friend's pocket.

"No."

"Why not?"

"Just let him see the phone," Golmer said.

"Shouldn't we be focusing on saying *our* goodbyes?"

"I have three hours! This won't take even three minutes!"

"You can't talk to her!" Bruce shouted.

"Why the hell not?"

Silence.

"If you don't fulfill a dying man's request then you might as well be pissing on their grave."

"She has a thing for Peter," Bruce blurted out.

"So what? It's not like they're married. Maybe there's still a chance."

"Give him the phone," Golmer was getting testy now.

"I can't, it's dead."

"Bullshit! I just saw you talking on it five minutes ago," Golmer stated.

Bruce took a deep breath.

"What's going on, really?" Terrance asked.

"I was on the phone with her. She needed help. I declined."

"What kind of help?" Terrance asked worriedly.

"She needed to get herself and others out of Saurian Safari."

"My god, Canton." Golmer shook his head. "What were you thinking?"

"Get me out of here. I want to be discharged."

"You can't. Who knows when the infection will become painful again. It could be unbearable," Bruce explained.

"We're not in a charter business," Terrance said. "We do missions. This sounds like the most important mission we've had. I'm not going to miss it."

Bruce reached forward and pressed a button on the wall. A nurse quickly came in.

"If he tries to leave, have him restrained. Tied down. I want security on him, at least one guard," he told her.

"I'm not sure I can. You don't have the authority."

"Then put him in a padded fucking cell."

"This isn't some barbaric asylum."

Bruce spun around and faced the woman. "Then I suggest you get someone in here to keep him tied up."

She searched his eyes for any sign of reluctance. He seemed serious. "I'll try my best. I'll handle this."

"Golmer. You stay with your brother.

"You can't fly the chopper alone!" his friend replied.

"Just leave me one of our radios," Terrance said suddenly. "I want updates."

Looking over his shoulder, Bruce nodded. "Deal."

***

He was aimless. The hallways were still flashing red. Peter Denning was afraid he was not going to make it in time to save everyone. He had already failed his friends. Now the guests and employees were at risk and there may in fact be nothing he could do.

As he rounded the corridor, the lights suddenly flickered on.

"What game is that bastard playing now?" he said to himself.

Alister Ward had deceived them all. He had hidden right under their noses and no one suspected a thing. It was a case of bad intuition on Francis' part. The man trusted too many people.

Peter thought back on Francis. The poor man had been killed by his own discovery. He was not a bad person. A bit clueless and impulsive perhaps. He guessed that was just how entrepreneurs were. They were all so excited to get their products, or in this case exhibits, out to the world. Show them what they had. It was a matter of life and death now.

The man should have just left them in the Congo, Peter thought as he began to hear commotion up ahead. He ran for a set of doors and realized he was near the cafeteria.

"Oh, thank God!"

He shoved the doors open and stumbled into a scene of escalating chaos. Several of the guests were arguing with Megan while the rest were sitting at the tables, shaking with fear. Peter spotted Sarah who was talking to a familiar face.

The reporter.

"What are you doing here?" Peter asked as he approached.

"I came to warn you. There's been betrayal on your staff," Catt spoke urgently.

"I know. Alister shut everything down. I don't know what his plan is or why he's doing it. I'll take the power being on for now though."

"That fucking creep!" Sarah shouted. "He's already cost a kid's life."

"Who?"

"Roy Hayes," Sarah continued. "We don't know where his brother is. Mr. Hayes is distraught. He just watched the Spinosaurus eat his own son."

"It's not just the Spino," Peter said suddenly. "The Utahraptor are out too."

"Where's Francis?" he heard Megan shout over to him over the angry small crowd.

Peter did not say a word.

Megan shoved past the guests and hurried over. "Where's my husband?"

"I'm sorry, Mrs. Conners."

"What? No! What the hell happened?"

"Alister. He let out the Utahraptor. We tried to fight them off but Francis sacrificed himself so I could get away. He died a hero."

Megan's lower lip quivered.

"We need to leave!" Ms. Kragle snapped at them.

"We can't!" Catt spoke up. "The men at the dock are also responsible for the dinosaurs being out. They may have done it inadvertently, but they *are* working for Alister. That much I can guarantee."

"So what do we do?" Sarah asked.

Catt did a quick intake of breath. "I tried to get ahold of the pilots you guys are friends with. They denied their service. I'm afraid we're on our own."

"Those bastards!" Peter snapped.

"Forget them!" Megan spoke up suddenly. "We need to find my daughter and anyone else in the facility and get somewhere safe."

"Where's safe?" Catt asked.

No one responded.

***

Genetic memory of the tyrannosaur hunting pattern was passed down to them both. Their offspring, in turn, inherited the traits. The Congo was their home for many years. After being thrust into their new environment, they began trying new techniques.

Across from them, they watched as the Spinosaurus escaped and tore apart those morsels. It made them salivate. It was as if they had been craving human flesh for millions of years despite them never encountering them before arriving.

They watched as it charged down the hall after the other fleeing prey. The very fact that it was free enraged them. Why did it deserve to be out? The male tyrannosaur walked up to the glass. There was normally some kind of force keeping them at bay from breeching their new environment. An electrical current that made them feel uncomfortable.

It was off.

Backing up, the bull tyrannosaur prepped its stance. He did not second guess the deprecations of what he was about to do. The thought never even crossed his mind. Instead, he charged for the barrier. As he neared, he lowered his head to allow full impact onto his thick skull.

He collided with it; the impact was so tremendous that it shook the frame of the entire glass panel. Cracks started to appear. They spread out like a spider web. He shook his head to try and fight off the headache he was enduring. As he turned in retreat, his long tail swept up and smashed into the glass, shattering it into millions of tiny fragments.

As the bull tyrannosaur marched back over, his mate and offspring followed. Taking the first step, his feet touched the tile flooring, the glass stabbing into them. They felt like tiny pricks, and he paid them no mind. They were free now, just like the rest.

CHAPTER NINETEETN

They were close.

Jason Woo led Daisy and Ugros through the complex with determination. He was looking for a safe exit but also kept his mind on the neanderthal. He was not used to these conditions or environment. He feared if Daisy were not here, he would lose control and hurt himself or someone else. There was no telling the extent of his strength. Not when he was so docile towards others. His passive aggressive nature was the complete opposite of Hysyr.

Daisy too was worried for the safety of everyone. She did not know what she was getting into. Ugros was from another place and might as well have been from another time. His genetic structure was much different and more disfigured than their own. She had wondered if it was even a form of disfigurement or if he was supposed to look the way he did.

Ugros could sense her unease and motioned closer to her. He had to protect her. He had to protect anyone inferior than him. He was born to love unlike a majority of his tribe. Things were going to be different. A semblance of change was already working through his thought process. He was considering what the implications of being with Daisy would entail. He knew she was different but that did not make him care for her any less.

The three turned towards a pair of doors that read control room. "Wait here," Jason said.

"We should keep going," Daisy suggested.

"I need to try and get help. There's a sat phone situated at each desk. If I can get in there and get one, we'll have a way out of here."

Daisy looked unsure.

"We also need to prepare them for Ugros. I don't want any unnecessary assault inflicted upon him. They need to know what to and what not to shoot at," he explained.

She hung her head low. "Okay. We'll come with you."

"No."

"You need extra protection."

"Can you even shoot a gun?"

"No, but we've got him." Daisy gestured over to Ugros with her eyes.

"If he can even fit through the doors."

After a few attempts, Ugros ducked underneath the doors, and they made their way inside. Jason immediately detected the fowl odor. Then he saw the blood.

"What happened here?" Daisy asked.

"Someone's been attacked. I presume killed."

"Where are the phones?"

'They're over here. We keep one here and one inside the base of the control room."

He looked around, his light shining on random objects that were anything but a communications device.

"Maybe it fell?"

He braved a look down at the floor. If there was more blood, he was not sure the person could have survived. His answer lay ahead of him.

A pair of legs were sticking out from behind a desk. The person was wearing black pantlegs and matching shiny shoes.

"Oh, God. It must be one of the guests."

"What would a guest be doing in here?" Daisy inquired.

Jason suddenly froze.

"What is it?" she asked.

He did not respond. It was not until she took a few steps forward and the sound of her high heels caught his attention, snapping him out of his temporary shock. "Don't come over here."

It was too late. She stumbled upon the sight of the mangled remains of her father.

"No!" she cried out.

Ugros approached quickly at the sound of her scream. He wanted to comfort her. He only made it a few feet before one of the Utahraptors slammed into him.

Jason spun around as he saw the scene unfold. He did not see the light turn on in the computer room. Daisy did. Inside, she saw Alister with a somewhat pained expression. He turned on the intercom and spoke.

"I'm sorry but, you'll have to go too."

"What?" Daisy's voice trembled.

"It's how it's got to be, cutie."

A loud clashing sound caught her attention, and she spun around. The sight of Ugros doing battle with one of the Utahraptor was horrible. He was already cut up, blood trickling down from his wounds.

"Get away from him!"

Another Utahraptor screeched in response. It was slowly approaching her and Jason. Neither had seen, let alone heard it coming.

Jason raised his rifle and trained his sights on the creature. It ducked down, causing Jason to miss. It then sprung forward. Jason and Daisy ducked out of the way and it landed between them, sliding across the floor.

Ugros grabbed the dinosaur by the jaws as they parted to snap at him. The terrible teeth cut into his hands as he fought to keep its mouth from closing over his fingers. He let out a roar that rivaled *King Kong* and began to use his strength in his right arm more. Soon, there was the sound of cracking bone as the animal's mouth was pushed back, forcing it apart from the lower jaw. Blood shot out like a hose with a hand continuously being placed over it. It kept pumping as the Utahraptor fell to the floor.

Jason grabbed Daisy by the arm and guided her over to Ugros. "We have to get out of here."

"We can't leave my dad!"

"We don't have a choice. Let's go!" Jason argued.

The second Utahraptor had regained its footing, rose off the ground, and began to charge for them. Jason raised his rifle and wasted no time aiming. They were catching on too quickly to waste time trying to line up for his shot. He fired, hoping for a lucky hit. The bullet grazed the top of the dinosaur's skull, causing it to stumble forward onto the ground.

"Let's go!" He pulled at Daisy.

Suddenly, they heard another screech. They turned and saw the third and final Utahraptor over by the doors. It rose high up on its haunches and stared down at them, saliva dripping down its chin.

Daisy and Jason began to slowly back away. They both looked around. There were not many other options for escape. There was a door to their right, but Jason had a feeling Alister would have locked it. The power had been out too, possibly causing a short circuit. Daisy tried to start for the door, but he grabbed her arm. She looked at him as he shook his head.

The Utahraptor stood there, observing them. Jason wanted to believe it was simply deciding on what to do but he knew it was obvious. It was patiently waiting for them to flee. There was only one other option now. He reached into his pocket and fished out a round. The dinosaur took a step forward, ready to strike as soon as he had it in the chamber. He was not sure if he should even try. The clicking noise would be its cue to attack.

Before either had a chance to do anything, the ground below them began to shake. Daisy turned and saw the bloodied Ugros charging for the Utahraptor. His fist slowly rose high. The dinosaur was taken aback at first but then turned its attention to the hulking brute. It lowered down on its haunches and then pushed itself off the ground, leaping high and soaring through the air. It came down with a terrible claw, ready to slice Ugros from neck to groin. It did not have time to calculate its attack nor see Ugros' other hand hook around. He caught the predator by the throat and held it aloft.

Clawing, screeching, the Utahraptor tried to rip itself away. As it did, Ugros tightened his grip. He then lowered it to face level and drove his fist into the front of its snout. His knuckles plowed through and crushed the cartilage in its nostrils. He kept going, pushing it further into the prehistoric creature's nose. Blood began to erupt and gush over its arm. He then retracted and observed his action. The face of the Utahraptor was barely recognizable save for a few teeth and the eyes were still intact. One tried to blink but there was some muscle bulging right below its socket, restricting its ability.

He then let it fall to the floor. It did not get up. It bled.

The last Utahraptor had stopped its advancement when it saw its sibling's skull being caved in. It turned and ran further into the control room.

"Let's get out of here!" Jason cheered.

Daisy ran over to Ugros. He was bleeding all over but was still able to look at her with that same affection. She put one of his massive arms over her shoulder and aided in getting him out of there. Jason did the same and the three made their way out of the room.

Alister's finger hovered over the button. The door could have closed and locked permanently. He had no objection when it came to keeping them away from the others. Part of him wanted to do just that. The thought of Daisy being torn apart sat well with him at first but now, seeing how beautiful she looked in that light pink dress with all those glowing diamonds on it. She was dazzling to say the least.

He watched them go and then regretted it. He knew there was no escape. The only transportation was working for him. Their lifelines were cut. Service for cellphones was out the window once he shut down the power and, in turn, the routers. The landlines were in this very room, and he had them.

There was the possibility of satphones, and he wished he invested in a jammer. No one on staff had one that he knew of. There was never a need. They had Wi-Fi and connections to the outside world.

A vibration made him reach into his pocket and pull out his pager. It was an obsolete device but perfect for these kinds of situations. What he read was discerning though.

Turn power on. Trouble.

"That's not good."

He looked over the controls. He would allow power to be restored but only to certain parts of the building. He had to get in contact with them by phone. He could not risk using the landline. They would be able to trace that and link the whole plan back to him.

There was a button for two rooms. If he turned the power on to them, he would have access to his connections. He would also be turning on the power to the cafeteria. Everyone was in there. It was true they already had the light from outside and it would only take a few minutes. When it was nighttime though, he would have to stay silent. Unless everyone was already dead.

Pulling out his phone, he pressed the button and quickly began to dial.

***

A perfect predator, the Utahraptor found itself currently running away from its prey. There was no honor in its mind, no sense of dignity. It was simply trying to survive in this world so far from its own.

Its wide strides made it practically leap with each step. There was indeed urgency to its maneuvers as well as its own personal mindset. It had to escape from the colossal figure that crushed its sibling's face, causing it to cave in with one powerful blow.

Slowing its pace, the Utahraptor came to a sudden stop when it heard commotion and sensed a desirable odor. The drive of self-preservation was not as strong as before. The carnivorous side of the dinosaur came to the forefront. It smelled the fresh meat not far from where it was. The swelling notion of its stomach groaning took over every thought of its exodus and it changed direction.

The noise was getting louder as it hurried over. There were other sounds as well. They were artificial. Knives were being sharpened against each other. Glass clanked; machines groaned. It was a bustling area. One that was filled with many lifeforms. Each one emitted a kind of concern. Something was wrong and they felt lost.

Weak prey. Inferior to the gargantuan that killed its sibling but not without defenses. Some carried weapons that were similar to ones its captors pointed at it back home. It knew that if it moved fast enough, they would not be a problem.

It pinpointed one lifeform that was making its way towards him. He was oblivious to its presence. There was no doubt he would be the easiest target. After all, he was alone. His companion was over by the counter, looking at everyone. There was no better time.

The Utahraptor scurried along the wall towards the small establishment. It moved with such finesse that it barely made a sound as it darted twenty feet across the tile floor. There was no time to waste. It slipped inside just as the man entered.

Needlelike teeth clamped down around his neck. His head was then tugged in one direction, snapping. His spine followed and cracked. He never even made a sound.

CHAPTER TWENTY

What chaos brings.

Megan Conners was on the verge of having a panic attack. The guests were bombarding her with more questions while she dealt with the mental grievance that her husband was dead. He may have thrown caution to the wind, but he was a good man. He was a successful entrepreneur, and they had a healthy relationship. They were a rarity couple in the world of celebrities.

I wish I could have told him how much I loved him. Just one last time.

The last legacy they had was Daisy and she could not find her. She began to fear the worst. She was dead, there was no other way about it. She had been gone too long, and they would stumble across her body on their way towards the exit. If they did, she knew she would not be able to cope with it.

Peter was over by Sarah. The two were standing by a display about the Saurian Safari. It was a map detailing the layout of the area. Their expressions made it seem they were hopeless. Safety was not guaranteed anywhere. Every building had several exit points. The further inside they could go, the more it either led to a dead end, or dinosaurs.

"This is insane!" Mr. Hayes shouted. "There has to be a way out of here."

"There is. It's out there," Eugine stated as he pointed towards the glass windowpane.

"They're out there! We'd die just like my son," Mr. Hayes shouted. "There is no way I'm going out there."

"Not so computer generated now, are they Mr. Hayes," Ms. Kragle smirked.

"Fuck you, you ugly hag!"

"There's no time for this!" Peter argued. "We have to figure out a plan. We can't stay here. They'll get in for sure. We are probably better off making a run for it if I'm being honest."

"Run where?" Catt looked at him, fearful and unsure.

"If we can get to the jeeps, we can try to make it to the compound. It was a refueling station. So, if there's any gas left, we may be able to travel far," Sarah explained.

"What do we do when we run out of gas?" Milton looked at his father and then to the rest.

Sarah took a deep breath. "There is an old observatory. It was used for studying birdlife in containment. If the structure is still sound, we can barricade ourselves in. Hell, maybe there's even cell service on another part of the island. We need to try something!"

"I'll take my chances here," Ms. Kragle chuckled. "I'm not marching through the jungle for a possibility. I want assurance."

"There is none now," a voice called from across the cafeteria.

Everyone turned to see Jason. He was covered in perspiration and seemed to have shaved ten years off his life from fright alone.

"Where have you been?" Megan shouted. "Where's my daughter?"

"She's safe." Jason looked around. "Everyone, I need to have your attention please. We have an ally. He can offer protection from these creatures."

"Who or what is it? Another one of your dinosaurs?" Mr. Hayes scoffed.

"There's no need for snide remarks." Jason gave him a stern look. "He just might save your life at some point."

"Who?" Ms. Kragle was getting impatient.

"I must warn you. He is probably not what you are expecting. He is a…"

Ahhhh!

Akira had only been with the company for a few months, and, in that time, he had no complaints about his job. They paid well and were courteous to his needs. The only blemish in his profession at the sushi joint was his coworker, Hakata. It was not that he was a bum, leeching off the kindness of the Conners. He was a snoopy individual with more secrets than he claimed others had.

He had just left to put something in the freezer. Akira stood behind the counter and watched as everyone panicked. There was something going on. Something big. *He sure has been gone a long time.*

A decision was made by Akira that he himself was not too elated about. He had to check on his coworker though. Even if he was being annoying. He thought about last week when Hakata claimed that the food was no good and blamed Akira for sloppy preparation. Francis would not hear it though. He knew that both men were top chefs and realized it was just bad fish brought to them by the trade ship. As Akira approached the plastic flaps that covered the freezer doorway, he was reminded how much he despised them. They were an inconvenience and always seemed to intentionally fall to get in one's way.

It stepped into view. By way of shadow, Akira realized it was one of the dinosaurs. It was in the freezer. He assumed it was searching for a free meal but did not want to take that chance. Instead of trying to intimidate the animal, he turned the corner and made his way for the exit. The door was open, which is how Akira presumed it got inside.

Something was on the ground. He did not see it until his foot bumped into the limp body. Without thinking, he looked down and instantly wished he had not. It was Hakata.

"Ahhhh!" he cried out and ran back the way he came.

Passing by the freezer, the dinosaur pushed through the flaps and snatched Akira by the head. The intense pressure was torturous as it carried him out towards the serving counter. All he could do was scream and grab at the thing's face. His eyes bulged out as tears of blood spilled down his cheeks. His agonized wailing became less frequent. There was a snap, pop, crack and he went silent.

Everyone in the dining area turned and saw Akira's head come off his body. The sound was wet and mushy as it left behind a trail of meat and the ragged stump where his head used to be.

Chaos erupted. Minds, frazzled by the sight of one of the cooks being decapitated, were thrust into survival mode. Several of the guests were rigid with fear. Milton seemed to be the fastest to react. He wasted no time slipping from his father's hold and running towards the glass doors. Eugine did not register his absence until a few seconds had passed.

The boy was in flight mode. He had never seen anything so horrifying. Sure, he'd seen it in movies but never in real life. The worst part about it was that it looked just like it did in the movies. Blood erupting from the stump, the face, frozen in an eternal permanency of shock. He had not watched it for long. A lot was left to his imagination. He could have sworn the severed head blinked at him.

Pushing past the glass doors, Milton was the first outside and the first to be grabbed. Mr. Hayes had turned just in time to see his small body being lifted off the ground and carried into the air.

"What the hell was that?" he asked no one in particular.

By this time, Eugine was looking for Milton. He had not seen which direction he went. He had a feeling he went to hide under a table and began to peer under each of them.

"What was what?" Peter asked.

"Something just came by and picked that kid up."

Eugine dropped the tablecloth he was holding up to see under one of the tables and stood straight. "What?"

"Your boy! He was taken by some flying creature!" Mr. Hayes' face showed disbelief, as if he could not understand what had just happened before his very eyes.

"Forget him! We have to run!" Ms. Kragle shouted.

A terrible screech could be heard. The dinosaur had dropped the body of the cook and was now scanning the area.

Jason watched as it locked eyes with Aly Jane over at her station. It hopped on the countertop and then leapt off. Using its three-inch claws, it swatted at the guests. It hit a man across the cheek, sending blood and flesh flying and splattering all over Ms. Kragle. She was more disgusted than anything. Another guest, a woman, was slashed across the belly. Her intestines hit the floor with a wet, slimy splat.

"Aly!" Jason screamed as he watched the Utahraptor making its way closer.

He raised his rifle and followed the trajectory of the dinosaur. Once he felt confident that the sights were lined up perfectly, he took the shot. At the last possible second, Eugine shoved past him and ran for the doors. He missed the mark, and the bullet hit the ceiling right above the monitor in the center of the room.

Wasting no time, Aly searched for a weapon. Running a beverage establishment, there was not much to choose from. She grabbed her favorite blender and chucked it at the dinosaur. It landed short, exploding into large fragments that the Utahraptor simply hopped over. All was lost and she sprinted towards her fridge off to her left. It only took several steps. Half of them were used to moving out of the way to get the door open more. She did not waste time and hurried inside. The door was not heavy, and she began closing it with ease.

A long scaly arm reached inside. The talon-like claws scraped across her belly but she did not pay much attention to it. She got the door to slam over the creature's arm and it responded by pulling back. The door shut and she suddenly began to feel weak.

Jason approached the counter just in time to see the Utahraptor retract its scaly arm from the walk-in fridge. Its claws were coated in red. He feared the worst and shouldered his rifle. The dinosaur was reeling back in pain. He figured the door shut on its forearm.

"Eat this!" Jason fired a shot, but it went wide.

The impact of the bullet slamming into the glass container caused shards and juice to go everywhere. The Utahraptor paid no attention. It did not flinch or react. Instead, it lowered itself into a crouching position and snarled. They both knew what was coming.

He aimed and pulled the trigger. A resounding click signified that the weapon was empty. His face turned pale as he watched the Utahraptor leap through the air, soaring over the counter. There was no time to react. Jason tried to turn and run but tripped over himself. It landed over him, legs on either side of his own.

Lifting one foot, it placed its scythe-claw on his back. The pressure Jason felt digging into his shoulder blade grew more and more intense. He let out a blood curdling scream. The worst was yet to come. He knew it. He had seen the reports of attacks and fatalities these creatures caused. He would be just another mangled body for people to use as a precautionary warning.

The unmistakable sound of a projectile whizzing by above him could be heard. Then, a splattering sensation came down like rain on his back. The pressure quickly lifted off him. Jason wasted no time turning over onto his rear, using his hands to push off the ground. What lay before him was the Utahraptor. Half its face was gone and there was a gaping hole in the center of its head.

"Jesus," Jason whispered.

"Count your blessings!" Peter ran over to him. "Because not even a cat would get that lucky. Nine lives and all."

Sarah quickly approached as well. Together, the siblings lifted the injured man off the ground.

"Are you alright?" she asked.

Jason nodded. "I think so. Where's Aly?"

Peter looked at Sarah who shrugged. He then made his way around the counter and found blood on the ground. It had been smeared as if it had been stepped and slid in. The closer he got, he realized it was mostly coming from the fridge. It did not look good at all. There was a dark puddle seeping from a crack in the door.

A weak voice escaped from barely parted lips. "Is it gone?"

He made his way over and slowly reached forward for the handle. As he pulled, more blood seemed to pour out. Aly was there, pale as a ghost. She was clutching her stomach. It dawned on Peter that she was holding her intestines in place.

“Don’t let,” she coughed. “Don’t let Jason see me like this.”

“I don’t know what to do,” Peter stated.

“It’s too late for me.” A single tear inched down her face. “Save...”

She began to hyperventilate.

“Save who?” he asked as her whole body shook.

“Everyone you can.” Her words were spaced out and hoarse, but he understood.

Peter then reached out and picked up her hand softly. At first, she was particularly strong, a death grip. Then it began to soften as she slouched over. Finally, her other hand fell, and her guts plopped to the floor.

There was an uneasy silence between man and corpse. He looked into her dead eyes but did not cry. He wondered if Terrance was looking at Golmer the same way at this very moment. The siblings were inseparable. Peter realized then and there that he had failed them. Aly never stood a chance at being saved. It was going to be a hard pill to swallow for Jason.

“Is she gone?” Peter heard Jason’s voice call from outside.

What felt like a minute was really only a few seconds before he responded. “I’m sorry, Jason.”

There was silence at first but then Peter could hear the sobbing. He wished he had been as sympathetic to those he cared about as Jason was to Aly. He then stood up and marched out of the beverage establishment. “Let’s get out of here.”

‘What about the Spinosaurus?” Sarah asked fearfully.

“We’ll deal with that thing if it comes after us.”

Sarah looked around the room. There were only a few guests left, including Ms. Kragle. Eugine and Mr. Hayes had left the mess hall. She was not sure where they had gone off to. All she knew was that Milton had been taken, and Eugine was probably looking for him.

“I’m not moving from here!” Ms. Kragle snapped at them.

“We don’t have a choice. It’s not safe,” Peter stated.

“You took care of that dinosaur rather easily,” one of the other guests piped up for the first time the whole tour.

“It killed at least two people before I did though. I’m not sure where Hakata is but I’m pretty certain he’s in the same boat as Akira’s lifeless body over there,” Peter explained.

“Real tasteful,” Ms. Kragle scoffed.

“We have no chance against that mega lizard out there!” the same guest said.

"We might." Jason attempted to grab hold of one of the chairs at a table. "We do have an ally."

"Oh?" Ms. Kragle's eyebrow arched.

"Daisy," Jason called out to her. "Bring him out."

Ms. Kragle and the others waited impatiently. Megan looked up, eager to see her daughter. She was not sure how she was taking the news of Francis and wanted to be there for her.

Daisy came out first. She turned back and nodded. The hulking mass of Ugros barely fit through the doors as he answered to her beckoning.

"What the hell is that thing?" Ms. Kragle shouted.

"He would have been the last exhibit on the tour," Jason said weakly.

No one responded as Ugros came further into the room. He turned, noticing Jason, and made his way over. The injury the man had sustained was bad but not fatal. It was clear he would need medical attention fast. Ugros leaned over and, along with Sarah, helped the man to his feet.

Megan hurried over, her long sky-blue satin dress gliding over the blood-stained floor. She reached for Daisy who returned the gesture. They embraced. "I'm so sorry."

"Dad. He's…"

"I know." Megan clung to her daughter.

CHAPTER TWENTY-ONE

It was all falling apart.

Simple plans seemed to always come with a caveat for Peter. He had brought ideas to the table. People listened to him; he had friends. They were becoming less and less the more time passed. Others died on his watch. Golmer and Bruce were likely to never speak to him again. Terrance, he was not sure if he even could. The dead don't talk. Peter's mind was made up by now. He was never seeing his friends again.

Undecided on how the next course of action should be implemented, he was deep in thought. Making his way around the counter, he looked at Jason whose lucidity was slowly slipping. They needed to get out of there. There were only so many options to do so but it was a must.

One guest, an Asian man dressed in a black tuxedo and with equally dark hair slicked back, began shouting as he came running towards the group. Peter recognized the man as the one who argued with them alongside Ms. Kragle. He was practically tripping over himself now. Stumbling over bodies and slipping in slick crimson plasma.

Those who remained looked at him with confusion. Some did not budge while others backed away. There was something wrong with the look in his eyes. It was as if he saw the devil himself. Whatever the reason, people were preparing to flee.

"It's a big one!" the man screamed. "It's coming down the hallway."

"What is?" Peter asked.

"How the hell should I know? They're your dinosaurs!"

A sudden roar shook the interior of the cafeteria. Sarah recognized it instantly. "No."

"What? What is it?" Ms. Kragle was becoming hysterical.

"Spinosaurus?" Peter turned to his sister.

"No. But it is from the Spinosaurus family."

"Baryonyx?"

She nodded.

The guttural sound echoed across the ceiling. It created a wall of noise that made one of the guests, a young blonde man, tremble and relieve himself in his suit.

"What do we do?" Megan turned to them, still clutching Daisy.

"We head for the exit," the Asian guest said as he ran past them.

He pushed through the doors and was greeted by a rush of humid air. It was not from the elements. Rather the Spinosaurus' hot breath encompassed him as did its jaws. The prehistoric beast seemed to have come from the side of the building. It slammed down around his torso with its terrible teeth and dragged him outside. He was lifted off his feet as if he weighed nothing.

"We're going to die!" The blonde man began to cry.

"Everyone get outside!" Peter ordered.

"What? Are you crazy?" Ms. Kragle shouted.

"It's feeding at the moment. We have a chance!" Peter suggested.

"I don't like this!" Catt was beginning to show chips in her armor. She was used to reporting violent crimes, but this was a bit too much.

"We don't have a choice!" Peter said.

"Alright, everyone! Please follow Mr. Denning outside," Megan said aloud.

The blonde man was the first to run towards the door. Ms. Kragle and one other guest, an overweight man from Wall Street, were not budging.

"We have to go, now!" Sarah shouted.

"I'm not moving!" Ms. Kragle barked.

Peter looked and saw the blonde guest was already halfway across the open lawn. He was not sure if he would survive alone. "Everyone who's coming, make sure to stay behind me!"

By the time they began to make their way outside, Ms. Kragle and the Wall Street man were attempting to find a place to hide. No one looked back. Not even when they heard the businessman scream.

***

Alister Ward watched as the Baryonyx charged into the cafeteria and immediately scooped up the large man. It shook him to and fro. He could hear him scream. It sounded like his lungs were about to explode from his chest. He was surprised his voice could go as high as it did.

He then noticed Ms. Kragle trying to make her way around the dinosaur. She pressed against the wall most of the way. She then made a mad dash for the hallway. The tail of the Baryonyx did not drag across the ground but was rather more equal to its overall height. As a result, it smacked Ms. Kragle in the face and sent her flying against the wall.

"Ooff." Alister could not help but cringe and laugh.

She slowly began to get up. He managed to zoom in on her. Her nose was unnaturally bent to the right and one of her eyes was pushed in further than the other. Swelling had instantly begun. Blood poured down her face and onto her white fur dress.

"It's an improvement," Alister chuckled.

Zooming out, he noticed the Baryonyx was not going after her but rather running after the others.

"We're almost done here," he chuckled.

***

Everyone was on edge. Peter was up front while Ugros brought up the rear. The rest were sandwiched in the middle. Catt and Sarah were helping Jason along, Megan and Daisy stayed close together. Distant screams and roars could be heard. It left an uneasiness hanging over them like an insidious fog.

"Where are we going to go?" Catt asked Peter.

"We'll have to make it down to the beach. Is there a boat you came here on?"

"I took the ferry. Gerald and his crew are probably on their way here now."

"What is the conspiracy going on?" Megan inquired.

"Does the name Regenold Fielding ring a bell?"

"It sounds familiar."

"He was the former CEO of Worldly Ventures. He was informed of a plan he wanted no part of. About a week ago I received a file. It was given to me by Fielding. It contained documents that laid out a plan to ruin your attraction. They had managed to get someone on the inside called Alister Ward. I'm sure you are aware of him."

"Sniveling little shit!" Megan cursed.

"Yeah, that guy. Anyway, he's the man who is going to be responsible for Saurian Safari's downfall."

"I still don't understand. Why would Worldly Ventures send one of their own employees to the island, with his son no less, if things were planned to go south?"

"I'm still trying to piece everything together," Catt said.

Jason made a groaning noise. "That's nice and all, but where is this ferry?"

"It's over this hill and down by the water's edge," Catt explained.
"Let's pick up the pace!" Peter called back to them.

Mr. Hayes had watched everyone exit the café. They were going in a certain direction that he knew led to the beach. There, he was not sure if there was already a boat of some kind or people waiting for them. Either way, he would not be excluded from the rescue.

Eugine had gone off to find his son. For all anyone knew, the kid was already gobbled and gone. Despite this, the man had persisted in finding him. Whatever took the boy was large and reptilian, yet it flew. He began to wonder what other horrors were on the island that they were not privy to yet.

That hulking brute that brought up the ground from behind was some kind of human saurian. It looked as though he understood what was going on and the gravity of the situation. He presumed it was working with them to try and escape.

Soon, they were making their way up a grassy hill. Mr. Hayes knew he had the advantage. He could circle the area and make his way to the beach well before them, but he had to move fast. Quickly looking around, the brief survey yielded no signs of dinosaurs nearby. He stood up and began to run around the palm trees and shrubbery. There was a sense that he was in his own saurian safari now. This time though, it was out in the wild.

***

Golmer and Bruce were making good haste. If it were not for Terrance's reassurance, they would still be at the hospital. They piloted the Bell UH-1 Iroquois with ease as it hugged the coastline. They would be near Darken Island within the next ten minutes.

Both knew that there was a lot that could happen in that time. It clung to the back of their minds, nagging at them like a bad memory. The escalating chaos they were bound to enter into was exhilarating, if not frightening.

"We need to hurry," Golmer shouted over the radio.

"What do you think we're doing? Flying a jet plane? I can only go so fast," Bruce grumbled.

The jungle below was a green hellscape of nightmarish creatures. They could not see life down there, but it could be felt. Eyes watching them, unwelcoming of their presence.

"I'm going to take her over to the docks. I just hope we're there in time."

***

"There it is!" Peter shouted.

Everyone cheered, picking up their pace. A sense of relief swooped over them like a wave of positivity. Perhaps there was a way out of this horrific event.

Megan hurried towards the front of the line. She met up with Sarah who showed signs of fatigue from helping carry Jason. "I've got him."

"Thanks." Sarah smiled as she relinquished the injured man to her.

Catt hurried over towards the dock and fished out the keys from her pocket. She did not think of dinosaurs in the water. The potential was there. As she began walking on the planks, Megan and Jason close behind, she felt a sense of uneasiness.

Jason managed to get aboard and lay down. Megan hopped on, her dress nearly catching some of the piling. Then, she sat next to Jason.

As Catt began towards the ferry, a hand shot up and grabbed her around her ankle. She screamed as she fumbled backwards and into the water.

"Catt!" Peter shouted.

A few seconds passed but there was no sign of her.

"What happened?" Sarah shouted.

"I don't know." Peter began towards the embankment. "I'm going in though."

He took a few steps into the ocean. The further he went, the faster the incline. Soon, he was breast stroking towards where Catt was. When he was close enough, he dove. The saltwater stung his eyes at first, but they soon adjusted.

A low, gurgling grumble that was muffled underwater could be heard. He quickly looked around but there was no sign of a dinosaur. He looked upwards and soon had his answer. The ferry. It had been started and was now making a U-turn around the shoreline. Bringing his hands forward, he began making his way towards the surface. He felt a grip around his calf, and he looked down. It was Catt. She pulled him down and then pointed.

There was something there. The noise had been coming from the engine but there was another source that could make a similar sound. It swam with a grace Peter would have found majestic had it not been so terrifying.

The Spinosaurus was circling the boat now. Its sail was just below the surface. It knew how to keep out of sight. As the ferry drove further away, Peter and Catt decided it was safe to return to the surface.

"What are you doing?" Megan shouted at Mr. Hayes as he steered away from shore.

"I'm getting out of here!"

"We have to wait for the others!" she exclaimed.

"You want to swim back for them? Be my guest. You're lucky I'm even allowing you on this boat. I have to sue somebody for both my boys' deaths, though."

"You're going about this all wrong," Megan began. "It was not my husband's intentions for this to happen. There was a disgruntled employee and…"

"You should have performed better background checks then, I guess." Mr. Hayes shook his head. "You know what. Save it for my lawyers. I've got more important things to think about."

"Like funeral arrangements?" Jason stated.

Mr. Hayes glared over his shoulder. "What did you just say?"

Jason realized he had overstepped. The man was not all there and he himself was already badly injured and feeling woozy. "It was nothing."

"No, you goddamn jap! Tell me what you said or I'll," Mr. Hayes paused as he looked behind the boat, out on the water. "What's that?"

Megan turned and saw that something was making ripples in the water. Soon, a massive sail broke the surface. Wavelets trailed behind it as water rushed past its scaly hide. Then came the front, the head of a crocodile.

"No," Megan spoke softly.

CHAPTER TWENTY-TWO

It was tricky.

There was an art to it, trekking through the jungle. The idea was simple enough. Awareness of the surroundings and the general layout of the area sounded simple enough. To Eugine Ferrand, the thought of finding his son trumped everything else. His own safety did not matter to him anymore. Milton had to be alive. The jungle could have swallowed he himself whole, but Eugine was determined to find him.

It had been almost an hour since he was told his son was taken. He had not seen any blood on the ground from where he stood. This gave him the hope and drive to plunge into the greenery. Soon, he found himself running aimlessly through flora. It was not so thick that he could not see the grassy area beyond the tree line, but it was enough for him to get lost if he was not careful.

He had come upon his first sign of impressions a few minutes before. The ground had small claw marks. It was in a muddier patch, so they were easier to spot. Eugine figured that whatever took his son, some flying creature as he was told, stopped here for a brief reprieve. It was even more evident given that it was just one pair of tracks. It was clearly resting before taking off with his son again.

Why wouldn't Milton run given the opportunity? He began to panic. *He would not have just given up. Something's wrong!*

Then he heard it.

A loud screeching sound that was shrill and angry filled his ears. He had to cover them to block out the hellish noise. It was drawn out but not too long, just enough to annoy Eugune. He uncovered his ears and looked up to where the shriek originated from. It sat there, on a thick branch in the canopy above, looking down at him.

"They have flying dinosaurs too?" Eugine could not help but scoff at the idea.

The great winged predator was watching him like a cat looking into a pond. Much like fish to a feline, he was prey to whatever this monstrosity was. He began to back away. There was no certainty he could find a thick brush in time. He dared not take his eyes off the animal in fear of it disappearing suddenly. Instead, he reached behind him and waited until his hands brushed into trees or shrubbery.

Suddenly, the colossal creature seemingly let itself free fall from the branch. It barely parted its wings while it fell. The act helped hit land lightly on the jungle floor. It then began to walk on its wings towards Eugine.

He had never seen anything so hideous. It looked like some mutation. Some kind of pelican mixed with a crocodile. As the scaly saurian crawled over to him, he began to quicken his pace. Still walking backwards, he was not taking any chances. If he ran, he figured he could not outpace the avian reptile. Suddenly, he found himself stumbling over something. He hit the ground hard and looked to see it was some rotted old tree. His back and hands were covered in chunks of splintered wood. There was not time to worry about that though. It was closer now than ever before. He began to hyperventilate.

"Please! Don't!" he cried out.

There was no sign of understanding. It did not sympathize with him. Nor did it see anything in front of it other than a quick meal. The beak plowed into Eugune's chest without warning. Blood splattered around the circumference of the impact. His chest was caved in, and most of his ribs were broken.

He wheezed. "My son."

Both man and prehistoric animal stared at each other. One with desperation, the other with primal rage. It retracted its beak and then leapt forward on top of him. Its small, clawed feet had an impressive grip that lifted him off the ground and carried him higher and higher.

***

The patience of the great dinosaur was impressive. For the Spinosaurus, there was a sense that it was enjoying taunting its prey. It had been circling the ferry for a few minutes now. A massive sail in the crystal blue, the abnormally large hump presented itself to the three passengers. It was a reminder of where it was at all times. Death watched them from below.

Mr. Hayes was not as surprised by the hunter. He was annoyed, yes. The chance to escape was thinning like old hair. He needed to get out of there, away from Darken Island. The proper authorities had to be informed. Saurian Safari was a dangerous place. No one should have even humored the idea of bringing dinosaurs here, let alone endorsed it.

The baffling motion to proceed with the plan was something he would have to have his private eye look into. Something was amiss.

He continued watching the Spinosaurus. The ill-conceived plan to have a creature such as this anywhere near the public was downright insane. It was not the only one. Other dinosaurs were loose too. To Hayes, he had a rivalry with the Spinosaurus. It had killed his son and most likely his other son as well. He would have it destroyed the moment he got back to the mainland and found a phone that worked.

Suddenly, the sail disappeared beneath the water. Megan gasped. She was not sure if it had lost interest or was about to attack. She turned to shore and saw Daisy looking at her. Her petrified expression made her heart sink. *She can't lose both of us.*

"What do we do?" Jason tried to look up but was having trouble.

"Can this contraption go any faster?" Mr. Hayes made his way over to the consol.

"I don't think so! Don't push it too hard. You'll stall it," Megan explained.

At first, the shadow that fell upon the ferry made Mr. Hayes think rain was coming. It was just what they needed. He chuckled and looked up.

It was there.

The Spinosaurus loomed over them. Its beady red eyes narrowed onto Mr. Hayes and then looked up at the other two. Its upper lip curled slightly, and it let loose a guttural snarl.

At that moment, Mr. Hayes lost control of his bowels. He took a step back, which was his biggest mistake. The great creature's head snapped in his direction.

"Oh God," he whimpered.

He squeezed his eyes shut and prepared for the worst. Behind his lids, he could see a strong orange and figured the dinosaur had moved out of the direction of the sun. When no pain came, he dared to open one eye. The Spinosaurus was now turned away from them. It was facing the sky. There, amidst the blue skies, was a helicopter.

"Yes!" Megan cheered.

As if to further celebrate their rescue, the cockpit door opened, and a burly man sat there on one knee. He was cradling an M16 machine gun. He quickly opened fire, pelting the dinosaur with several rounds. Small red spots formed on its back. In response, it roared with defiance and slipped beneath the waves. The man continued to fire until he turned back to the pilot and nodded.

He then grabbed for a ladder and tossed it over the side. The pilot maneuvered towards the ferry until it was directly above it.

"Jason, you first!"

Megan was surprised when Mr. Hayes did not argue. In fact, he came over to help him up. It was not until it was too late did she realize why. He hurried over to the portside and shook him off, allowing the injured man to tumble awkwardly into the water.

"No!" Megan cried.

She ran over and searched for the water. There were signs of red but he had landed over a coral bed. It was hard to tell where he was. She then turned back and saw Mr. Hayes reaching for the ladder.

"You bastard!" Megan screamed.

He paid her no mind. His fingers were inches away from his escape rope. He figured he would commandeer the M16 and force the pilot to leave. The further he was from this horrible island, the better.

His fingers touched one of the bars and he managed to snag it just as the Spinosaurus snagged him. It bit down around his midsection. A scream erupted from his throat as did blood from the puncture wounds. He stood there, pinned by the crocodilian jaws. The beast bit down harder and blood shot out of his mouth as he went into a crimson coughing fit.

Megan could only watch helplessly as the Spinosaurus pulled him off the deck and into the water. She peered over the side and saw the dinosaur shake him back and forth. Repulsively, he came apart in two halves and she stumbled back.

"Get me out of here!" she yelled up at the chopper, tears in her eyes.

The Bell UH-1 Iroquois was soon positioned over her again. She then heard a splash and looked down. It was Jason, he had surfaced. She abandoned the ladder and ran over to the portside, quickly reaching over.

Jason was able to grab hold of her hand, but it quickly fell. He was growing weaker by the second.

"Don't quit now!" Megan shouted.

He felt he was done for. A similar fate to Aly's would befall unto him. There was no reason to even try. He peered at the helicopter. The thought of their escape was laughable. Even if everyone had gotten aboard, they would be shot down by the harbor master and his men. It was too late.

"She wouldn't want you to give up!" Megan was screaming at him now.

"I can't," Jason replied softly.

"Just try!"

He had tried to save Aly and failed. His thoughts were completely wracked with guilt. *Try telling that to Aly. I tried to save you, but I couldn't stop the damned dinosaur from killing you. Sorry.*

Tears welled up in his eyes.

"Ugros needs you. We all need you!"

Jason felt hopeless. Despite the slim chance of escape, he was not ready to give it his all. His strength was waning.

"Reach!" Megan screamed angrily.

It was not a mindset that moved him to put his arm out but rather his body. Some force did not want him to give up. It was guiding him to salvation. He managed to grip her hand again and felt her pull. She used all her might. The pain in his shoulder was excruciating. The saltwater stung and his whole back felt as if it were on fire.

He did not know how she did it but she managed to get him back aboard.

"Thank God I work out!"

"Yes," Jason smirked. "Thank God."

They both chuckled just as they were sent flying over the edge. The Spinosaurus had slammed into the hull and sent the ferry tilting at a ninety-degree angle. Megan was the first to surface. She felt Jason down next to her and grabbed him by his hair, pulling him up. She could hear her daughter screaming wildly for her.

"Swim!" Megan cried.

Jason struggled but Megan helped him along. They continuously pressed themselves, slowing most of the time. They made a decent pace here and there. Neither of them dared look over their shoulders.

The screams on the shore told them enough.

Megan felt the sand under her fingers first. They both then began to claw onto shore. It was odd that there were no helping hands to aid them. Megan looked up and saw why. They were not screaming because the Spinosaurus was close behind them. It was the Baryonyx, it had come outside and was charging for the shoreline.

Stuck in an unescapable position, they managed to work their way out a little. They were all too aware that another prehistoric predator was watching them just below the surface. The Baryonyx was about ten yards away now. It roared as its rancid breath filled the tropical air. Jason turned away. The foul odor was effective on his already weakening state.

Megan turned to him. "I'm sorry."

Jason looked down at the sand beneath him. The tide was kicking up small particles of soot, carrying and returning them to their spot. “We had no right to do this.”

She nodded. “I’m starting to see that now.”

They looked at each other and laughed. Their moment of euphoria was cut short when the Baryonyx’s jaws slammed shut over Megan. Her screams were muffled within its mouth. Jason heard sloshing behind him and saw the Spinosaurus making a b-line for the shore. He knew it was his time now and waited for the agonizing pain to begin.

To his surprise, the cavernous mouth closed around Megan’s lower half. The two mighty monsters were playing a morbid game of tug-o-war. Her screams were replaced with the sounds of bones breaking and flesh ripping. Her sky-blue satin dress was now stained red. Jason could only watch in horror as her body was stretched. It began to flatten around her stomach region. For a brief moment, she was as flat as a pancake and then she came apart, ripped into two juicy halves. Her innards poured out of her waist and torso and down onto Jason.

He passed out.

CHAPTER TWENTY-THREE

They watched in horror.

Two species of the swamp had consumed what was left of Megan. Much like Jason, Daisy had passed out. Ugros managed to catch her and carefully placed her on his shoulder. Now, the dinosaurs had focused on new targets. Each other. The Baryonyx slowly stepped back as the Spinosaurus emerged from the water. It was as if it were allowing the larger predator ashore for a more equal battle.

Snarling, growling, they stared each other down. Their defiance was evident. Even though they had shared a meal, neither one of them wanted the other there. The Baryonyx carefully took a step forward. Its opponent did not break its gaze. Despite the Baryonyx being smaller, it was faster. Proving its agility, its bloodied jaws parted as it took a wide step forward. The first impact was not what it had anticipated. The Spinosaurus ducked down onto its front haunches. As the Baryonyx's target turned from its foe's neck to the massive sail on its back, it felt a pain grow on its leg.

The Spinosaurus had bitten down onto its calf. Blood pumped out as it pulled back its leg, shredding flesh against teeth as it went. Throwing its head back, the Baryonyx let out a massive roar of pained agony. It then came back down, its front teeth sinking down onto the sail. This caused the Spinosaurus to release its grip and back away. The Baryonyx took a chunk of scaly hide with it.

Another stare off began. This time, they were enraged by the injuries they had sustained. They were nothing serious but the hot stinging sensation was enough to make them agitated.The Baryonyx was about to take another lunge forward. It was determined to kill this fellow predator.

Suddenly, the ground shook. It caused the dinosaur to stop dead in its tracks. Both turned towards the structures behind them. The glass windows were vibrating as if someone was playing a song over an obnoxiously loud stereo near them. The sun cast down on the panel, making it difficult to see inside. There was a great shadow there. It was seemingly inspecting the glass pane in front of it.

There was no sudden charge from a distance. The tyrannosaur broke through the glass as if it were walking through an open door. It shattered into millions of small chunks as the creature's foot stepped down onto the grass. The tentative motion was almost fearful, as if it had not been outside, away from the comfort of the containment, for all its life.

As it overcame the obstacle, the tyrannosaur made its way out onto the lawn. Following it was the female and their single offspring. The youngling was already taller than a man and possessed all its parents' attributes. It did not hesitate either, charging for the Baryonyx and Spinosaurus. Both dinosaurs were now facing them completely.

The female tyrannosaur let out a warning bellow. Her instincts were to protect her calf. It was also a warning to the other predators to not dare to attack it. The Baryonyx seemed to heed the threatening roar, backing away slowly. The Spinosaurus did not. It stood its ground as the juvenile rex trotted over to it.

"We have to get to the Huey!" Peter shouted over the commotion of the dinosaurs.

"We need to get Jason out of there!" Sarah yelled.

Peter looked over and saw the man.

"Alright. Sarah. You and Catt get Bruce to land over by the yard." He turned to Ugros and pointed at Daisy. "Keep her safe."

The humanoid seemed to understand. He gave a brief snort. It was good enough for Peter.

"Be careful!" Catt told Peter.

"You owe me more than an explanation for everything after all this is done." Peter stared at her. "Maybe over dinner?"

"We don't have time for this!" Sarah was screaming now.

She grabbed Catt by the wrist and dragged her off towards the entrance of Saurian Safari. All the while, Peter made his way over towards some nearby shrubbery. A pitiful cover but it was the best around.

It would have been an awesome sight, a mighty match between monsters, had Peter not been so focused on Jason. The man was facedown, and he couldn't tell if he was breathing or not. There was no clear indication that he was dead though other than the gash on his back and him not moving. He figured the injured man was trying not to draw attention to himself. Yet that saltwater would sting his wound like alcohol. *Tough bastard must be fighting it out.*

A massive tail swooped over Peter's head. It was the Spinosaurus. As far as he was concerned, it was the most malicious dinosaur they had. It seemed to take pleasure in killing. It was not about the hunt. To further prove his point, the great saurian bent over and snatched the tyrannosaur calf off its feet and shook it around.

This time, Peter looked up. It was horrible to watch. The juvenile dinosaur stood no chance as its tiny arms tried to claw at the predator's crocodilian jaws. They pressed down harder in response. It let out a hoarse croak and then stopped moving. He then looked over and saw its parents taking on a look of agony and rage as they charged for the Spinosaurus. Their foe tossed their youngling over towards the ocean where it landed on the shoreline with a wet smack. It then charged its new opponents.

Peter saw this as his chance. He had a clear opening and did not waste a second. He hurried towards the beach. Then, in an astonishing surprise, Jason looked up. He was groggy but managed to raise an arm for Peter.

The Spinosaurus struck first. It slammed against the male rex with its shoulder which sent it tumbling to its left. Then, with one quick snap of its jaws, it had the female around the neck. The buck rex managed to regain some of its stance and turned to face the Spinosaurus. Yet its tail came around and smacked him in the face. Falling against some tall trees, he fell to the ground. The trees crushed against the goliath's weight, snapping like twigs. A shard of wood punctured him on his side, into his ribcage.

Blood erupted from the buck's mouth. He tried to get up but slipped on the grass and the sliver of wood slid deeper. It was soon pressing against his heart. The male rex was panicking now. There was only one more attempt he could make. Failing would result in death. In a different maneuver, he used his powerful legs to roll onto his side.

All the while, the female fought the urge to give in. The Spinosaurus had her in a grip that she could not escape. It was tightening. The unbearable pressure caused her to wince. Her eyes closed in pain as she let out a weak roar of defiance.

Then, with one last press of teeth to skin, she felt her airways being blocked completely. Another would result in it collapsing all together.

Her vision was going dark. She tried to reach up but could not get ahold of the predator. A vain attempt at survival, she pushed forward to try and shake the Spinosaurus loose. The resistance only caused the dinosaur to loosen its grip slightly. She felt cool air fill her chest. She took the regained lucidity and whipped her head to the left, successfully shaking the Spinosaurus off.

With a terrible roar, it snapped back at her. This time, it bit down onto her snout. The tyrannosaur's incredible jaw strength allowed her to open her mouth up despite the Spinosaurus' futile attempt at keeping it closed. In response, it clawed at her neck. The razor-sharp nails were digging at her like a set of razorblades. Crimson plasma gushed out. Her veins pulsated, causing the river of red to stop and squirt over and over again. The Spinosaurus dug deeper, ripping through flesh as if it were butter.

Soon, it was deep enough that her arm began to hang loose. The strands of sinew were the only things keeping it attached. It then fell off completely at the elbow. She threw back her massive head and howled in shocked agony. A new sensation emerged from her neck. The Spinosaurus had sunk its teeth into it as she arched back.

Then, as soon as it began, it stopped. The Spinosaurus had released her. The female tyrannosaur looked down and saw her calf biting at its leg. It gnawed at it as if it were a mouse chewing through wood. It was focused on its task which distracted the Spinosaurus long enough to feel a tremendous pain rocketing through its body.

Teeth dug into its own neck. They were as hard as rock and sharp as a butcher's knife. They dug deep as the Spinosaurus managed to turn its head far enough to see its attacker. It was the buck. The male rex wasted no time in chomping down as hard as it could. There was no thrill in killing. No desire to take it slow. The tyrannosaur severed its jugular and kept going. With one mighty tug, the Spinosaurus' head came off. A stream of blood exploded from the ragged stump.

Peter and Jason were almost by the shrubbery when the fatality occurred. They had not paid much attention to it. Their focus was set solely on the open area over by the entrance to Saurian Safari. They did hear the gurgling growl of the Spinosaurus and noticed when it suddenly stopped. They heard the head come off with a crackling snapping sound. It was gruesomely appalling but they did not dare look.

Soon, they were past the small bushes and were making their way past the smashed café windows. Catt turned and saw them. She quickly hurried over.

"The chopper's landing soon! We need to hurry!" she shouted.

Both men called to her, but it was too late. The Baryonyx snapped its jaws around her waist and began to shake her around like a dog with their chew toy.

"No!" Peter screamed. "No! Goddamnit! No!"

She was only able to emit breathless squeaks. Blood spilled out of her mouth in a gratuitous manner.

A bullet shot the Baryonyx on the side of the head. It merely shook its prey harder. Several more well-placed shots hit around its cranium before it retreated.

Peter nearly dropped Jason.

"She's gone, man. We have to go!" the injured man told him.

"This can't be happening!" Peter stated, an unfathomable rage in his tone. "We have to go!" Jason repeated. "Or we'll all end up like her!"

The idea of meeting a similar fate seemed to drive Peter into carrying Jason the rest of the way. Both men were now entering the garden area that was mostly open save for some tropical shrubbery.

"Where's Catt?" Sarah asked.

"Just help me get him aboard," Peter told her coldly.

"No," Sarah said with an equally plain tone.

The helicopter landed and Ugros gently laid Daisy in the cockpit. Sarah and Peter did the same for Jason.

"Sorry, big guy!" Bruce called over his shoulder. "This bird won't be able to handle everyone's weight with you aboard."

"What are you saying?" Jason looked at him. "We can't leave him."

"We won't all leave if we try to fly off with him," Golmer explained.

Daisy was still unconscious. Jason thought about it. It was better to leave him now. If Daisy came around and did not see him, she would make a bigger scene than need be at the moment. He knew she could not lose anyone else. He struggled to push himself up. "I'll stay with him."

"No!" Peter snapped at him. "I've already had too many people die under my watch. I can't let you down too."

"I'll be fine."

"You need medical attention!" Sarah said.

"I'm sure I can find a first aid kit." Jason was beginning to scoot off the helicopter.

Peter pushed him back and then grabbed Sarah and hauled her inside too. Then he grabbed the door and slid it shut.

Sarah whirled around and screamed, "No!"

Bruce did not waste any time ascending. Soon, they were high in the sky. Golmer was holding Sarah around the shoulder.

"We'll come back for them!" Golmer told her.

As the Bell UH-1 Iroquois flew away from the island, Sarah could only watch as Peter and Ugros' figures grew smaller and smaller. Soon, Darken Island was fading from view as well.

CHAPTER TWENTY-FOUR

The battleground.

Peter Denning was once top dog in the world of mercenaries. He was a hunter, adventurer, and thrill seeker. Working at Saurian Safari had changed him. He had seen horrors he was accustomed to but, at the same time, it was new. Like going from seeing a relative pass on to a full-on car crash. The carnivorous carnage that had taken place would go down as the worst theme park slaughter in history.

He turned to Ugros and regarded him coolly. The hulking brute was watching the helicopter take off. There were signs of distress. Despite him being from another time, he showcased true compassion for Daisy. He was not sure how far she allowed him in but Peter figured it was full on consent.

Ugros looked back at him briefly. Deep guttural noises escaped his mouth. He was trying to talk but could not form the words properly. Peter patted him on the back.

"We'll get you to her. Don't worry, big guy."

From somewhere behind them, there came a familiar sound. Peter turned. *I hope they're not coming back!*

The distant sound of blades whirring was all too apparent.

Ugros turned as well just in time to see the black helicopter fly overhead.

"That must be Gerald," Peter started and then turned to Ugros. "We have to hide."

***

The Huey flew over the island awkwardly. The pilot, Gerald had learned was known as Masimo, was slobbish in his flight execution. The aircraft was continuously dipping forward and then jerking back up. Gerald wondered how many drinks the man had consumed or if he were somehow not an actual pilot.

"Where did you go to flight school?"

"Flight school? Yeah right, man! That's for newbies."

"So what experience do you have?" Gerald asked.

"Man, I was born to fly!"

"That's not what I asked." Gerald looked ahead. "Just take her down over by the open field. I spotted something down there."

"Yes, boss!" Masimo made a roundabout turn that was actually halfway decent. The updraft was almost nonexistent. The landing was smooth despite a few hiccups when touching down. The skids kept touching and then rising from the ground.

"Alright, men!" Gerald turned to the four other guys in the cockpit. "Do this and you'll earn big.

They were Masimo's gang but were all he had at the moment. Two of them were Hawaiian natives. He did not bother asking their names. The operation would have to go accordingly. Any issues and Alister and Worldly Ventures Corp. would not be happy. Still, he figured he would never see these men afterwards. Gerald's worker who recommended Masimo certainly had poor judgment on his friends.

Masimo's gang looked like regular street thugs. The only difference, if there really even was one, was that they were bulky with tattoos up the wazoo. Each of them held high powered tranquilizer guns. Gerald made it clear that no one carried a lethal weapon other than himself.

"Let's move!" Gerald swung the door open.

He was the first one to get out. The others followed closely behind.

"So, we're hunting animatronics?"

"What?" Gerald turned to one of the native born thugs.

"Well, Masimo said there were dinosaurs that needed to be stopped. I assume he meant animatronics. No way are dinosaurs a real thing anymore, right? I mean, this is just some mechanical shit created by the government. Right?"

Gerald took a deep breath. "They're the real deal."

"Bull crap!" another thug that looked like George Lopez but with an afro said.

"It's the truth. We need to sedate them. Then we'll call in an extraction team."

"I wish I asked for more money," the second native-born thug said.

"I heard that!" the last thug, a 50 Cent wannabee complete with gold chains around his neck, said.

The five men walked down to the garden area. Gerald immediately noticed the yard was brushed down like a huge gust of wind had pushed the plants in its direction. There were also marks in the grass. Long, thin, pole-shaped indents. Skids.

"They've escaped," Gerald said.

"Maybe not all of them," one of the native men pointed.

Up ahead were imprints in the ground. They looked like they belonged to a foot that was at least size fifteen. Next to them were barely visible yet smaller ones. They were heading back towards the complex.

"Let's move," Gerald said.

It became clear that things were not as they seemed the further they went along. There were bloodstains in the grass and more large footprints. These were even bigger than the humanoid ones in the garden.

"Looks like the dinosaurs are loose," the buff Lopez lookalike said.

"Yeah, and they're definitely not animatronics," the other native said.

"How can you be sure?" Lopez lookalike asked.

"Because animatronic attractions don't attack their fellow machines." He pointed over towards the decapitated Spinosaurus.

"Fuuuccckk!" Gerald said as he exhaled.

"What could do that to that?" Faux 50 Cent looked on in disbelief.

Gerald snapped back into focus. "C'mon, guys. We've got a job to do."

Continuing, they made their way over towards the fallen dinosaur. They found the broken window and climbed over the frame and inside the cafeteria.

"Lights on," Lopez lookalike said as he clicked on his flashlight that was duct taped over the tranquilizer gun.

Everyone followed the order. What sight was bestowed on them was ghastly enough to cause them all to inhale a quick whisp of shock.

"What the hell happened here?" Faux 50 Cent asked.

Gerald gulped. "They got out."

"Or were let out," one of the natives said.

"Either way, we're the clean up crew. Let's get them before they get us," Gerald explained.

They fanned out, searching the area for clues as to where the dinosaurs could have gone.

"Where did they get these things anyway?" the other native asked.

"It's not really of concern," Gerald said.

"Just making small talk."

Gerald was not given any indication that the creatures' habitat was classified. Just their existence until the time was right. He thought on it. It would not hurt to break some of the tension these so-called hardened men were experiencing.

"The Congo."

"Congo, my ass!" the same native said aloud.

"What do you mean?"

"Listen, man. I was like most kids. I was a dinosaur fanatic." He shone his flashlight on a dead dinosaur over by a beverage joint. "That there's a Utahraptor. Now. Why would there be a Utahraptor in the Congo? Given the name, they would be somewhere out west."

"What are you getting at?"

"This dinosaur didn't come from no jungle. If it did, it was put there."

A small noise could be heard. It sounded like a muffled rolling can. Their lights shot up at its source and they saw a glass bottle making its way across the floor.

They waited for some kind of response. A snarl. A growl. There was none. Gerald figured it was human. "Come on out, whoever you are."

There was no answer.

The other native kept his gun trained on the spot as he made his way forward. No one else was budging. He wanted to tell them to come along but a sense of prideful ego took over. He was going to get whoever or whatever was over there. He would draw first blood.

It scurried across the floor. The rodent, small and grey, covered its hairy body across the floor like a wind-up racecar. The native took a step back. "They really need to set some traps."

"Those were treats for the Utahraptors," an unfamiliar voice came from further back around the corner.

"Ward! Is that you?" Gerald called out.

No response.

"Whoever that is, you've got five seconds to show yourself or we'll come for you ourselves."

"Let's just get this joker now!" Faux 50 Cent said as he began to make his way over towards the native.

"Hold your horses!" Gerald placed a hand on the burly man's shoulder. "We need to take this slow."

He shrugged him off but did not move further.

The other native began to back up towards the juice establishment. Things were getting weird. Too weird. First real live dinosaurs. Even though they were dead now, the very idea of them roaming around in the present time was a daunting thing to accept. The other was this joker playing hide and go seek. Even if he was alone, there was obviously a plan he had concocted.

A faint feeling of overheating began at the back of his neck. He'd had these feelings before. Mostly when working out at the gym. This time was different though. It was as if hot air was blown directly onto him. Or hot breath.

He whirled around, his flashlight's beam landing on the sight of some hideous humanoid creature. It wasted no time in reaching for him. The native had never seen anything so otherworldly. He instinctively shot at it but forgot that the weapon he carried only held tranquilizer darts. The needle hit the leathery skin but did not stop it from advancing onto him. With minimal effort, it leaned forward. It opened its mouth and encompassed his head. Then, with a forceful tug, it decapitated him. There were bitemarks in his neck stump as blood gushed out.

The other native spun around and screamed for his brother. The Lopez lookalike turned to see the man's headless body fall to the ground. It was dark but the blood could be seen squirting out and heard splattering on the floor a foot from the body.

"Holy Mary!" he cried out.

Gerald knew the game. Whoever was herding them over had obviously set up a trap. He did not face the direction the other men did. Instead, he continued forward.

Several more shots rang out. They sounded like wisping wind as the darts projected out and struck the hulking humanoid. Gerald still maintained his steady progression towards the man that was somewhere in the darkness. He caught sudden movement. A shape running out from around the corner and towards one of the tables. Reaching down, he withdrew his pistol.

Peter was sweating profusely. Despite Ugros killing one of them, there were still four men at the very least. He had to find a way to handle the rest of them if they took him down. He heard the soft sound of the gunshots and realized they were either using small caliber bullets or tranquilizers.

One of the men was approaching and he abandoned his post. Making his way to the nearest table, he did not stop. He kept running while keeping low. Soon, he was halfway around the cafeteria. He could see the light outside. It was no longer as bright as it was. The sun was going down. They had flashlights. He did not.

He was close now He saw fragments of glass scattered around on the ground, where the male tyrannosaur had broken through the window. It was everywhere. Peter figured he would have to make his way back. If he stepped on any shards, his position would be compromised. He looked to the left. There was a door that led to the outside. It was an emergency exit though. At first, he was about to abandon the idea. The alarm would go off and he would not make it through before being shot. Then he remembered the power was off. It had been on briefly. Then, when everyone went outside, the whole park shut down again.

There was only one chance. He had to make it. The exit was right there. There were no second thoughts. He bolted for it.

An overly bright light came on. The entire cafeteria was suddenly illuminated, and he was completely exposed. He did not bother looking over his shoulder. Running was all he could focus on at the moment.

Small particles of concrete kicked up into dust around his head. He heard the gunshots and was nearly smacked in the face by the debris. If it got in his eyes or mouth he would be done for. He closed his eyes and charged for the door.

The alarm went off. He was free.

Before he could make it to the garden, he tripped over something. It was a large mass that was lying on the red-stained grass. He quickly shot up and looked. It was the Baryonyx. His adrenaline began to wear off and he examined the fallen dinosaur. He did not want to, but a nagging feeling came over him. Maybe Catt was still alive. As he approached the head of the carnivore, his suspicions were put to rest. A pair of legs were hanging limp in its jaws.

He did not know how to react. What could he say? She had come to Darken Island to warn and save them and now she was dead. He squeezed his eyes tight, fighting back the tears. Then, he pressed on.

Gerald was the first to go outside. He looked out into the garden and then over by the wide-open field. There was no sign of the man. He cursed under his breath. *Witnesses.*

He was not the only one either. Whoever took off in the helicopter had seen what had happened too. He was not sure how much they knew. Part of him did not want to either. The less to do with this mission, the better.

A cold, frail hand came down on his shoulder and he spun around.

"You son of a bitch. Don't scare me like that!"

It was Alister. He looked like a man who had experienced pure joy only to receive the worst news of his life. The dangling fruit that fell on his face, he wore like a bad yearbook photo.

"We need to move."

"What about the evidence?"

"There are still three tyrannosaurs and two Pteranodons out there. Not to mention the stegosaurus I have locked up in the barn."

"And what do we do with all the dead dinosaurs?"

Alister thought for a moment. "Do your boys also clean up?"

CHAPTER TWENTY-FIVE

The way things go.

It would be a long journey home. A warm embrace covered the Huey as the sun set. Sarah looked at Golmer and nodded her thanks. Jason remained on the ground but was now turned over on his stomach. The patchwork Sarah had done had been crude, but it would do for the time being. Daisy was just coming around from her collapse. She was delirious for quite some time. She did not even know where she was until they were halfway to the mainland.

Bruce had announced they were almost home over the headset. Sarah and Golmer were wearing one. Daisy was still too unpredictably out of it to manage a device on top of her head at the moment. Sarah stood up and sat next to her.

She was not all there. Her body trembled as shock overcame her. It seemed the memories of what occurred on the island were coming back to her like a punch to the face.

All she could muster was to look out the window. Below, the calm waves rolled over each other. There was peace below. A world untamed and barely touched by human interference. There was so much left to explore. The Congo was like that. Except it was a place that had hideous monsters.

"Did he make it?" she muttered.

Sarah figured she meant Ugros and placed a hand on her shoulder. "We're not sure."

Suddenly, she looked away from the window and at her with big teary eyes. "What do you mean you're not sure?"

"We'll go back for him," Golmer told them both.

"Who else did you leave behind?" Daisy asked bitterly.

"Peter is still there. He chose to stay to keep Ugros safe."

Deep sobs escaped her trembling lips. She looked down at Jason.

"Do you need any help with him?"

"No. He should be fine for now. Just relax. We'll be back soon."

She began to sink into her seat.

"What the hell!" Bruce shouted suddenly.

Golmer pointed out the window. “Oh shit! Not again!”

Sarah and Daisy looked out and saw the pair of Pteranodons flying towards the Huey. They seemed to be homing in on them.

“What can we do?” Sarah asked.

Checking the mag on his M16, Golmer found there was not much left in the way of ammo. “Hopefully it’ll be like shooting fish in a barrel!”

He then quickly slid the door open and aimed.

The two flying reptiles looked up and then adjusted their trajectory. Soon, they were soaring over the aircraft. They came into Bruce’s view who was taken aback.

“What are they doing? Where are they going?”

“Wherever they go, we have to stop them!” Sarah shouted.

Daisy looked down at Jason. “We need to get him to a hospital first.”

Bruce thought about it. “Alright. We’ll touch down at the first hospital we see. Then, afterwards, we have to alert someone.”

“Why can’t we just handle it?” Bruce held up his weapon.

“I don’t think it’s just our problem anymore.” Jason weakly looked up.

Sarah stared out as the Pteranodons approached the coastline. “We took from nature. Now she’s taking back.”

The End

CHECK OUT OTHER GREAT DINOSAUR BOOKS

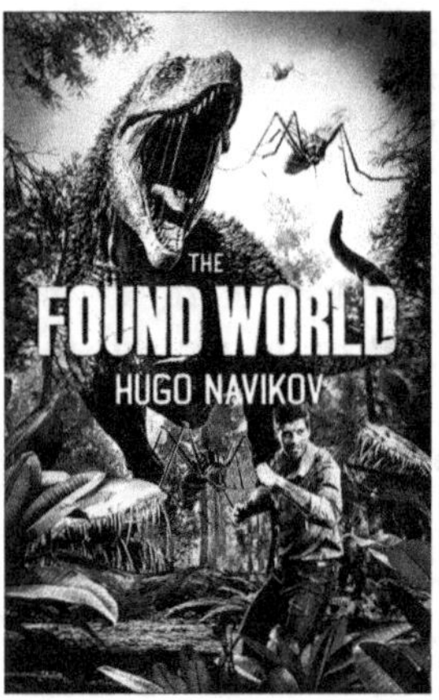

THE FOUND WORLD
by Hugo Navikov

A powerful global cabal wants adventurer Brett Russell to retrieve a superweapon stolen by the scientist who built it. To entice him to travel underneath one of the most dangerous volcanoes on Earth to find the scientist, this shadowy organization will pay him the only thing he cares about: information that will allow him to avenge his family's murder.

But before he can get paid, he and his team must enter an underground hellscape of killer plants, giant insects, terrifying dinosaurs, and an army of other predators never previously seen by man.

At the end of this journey awaits a revelation that could alter the fate of mankind ... if they can make it back from this horrifying found world.

HOUSE OF THE GODS
by Davide Mana

High above the steamy jungle of the Amazon basin, rise the flat plateaus known as the Tepui, the House of the Gods. Lost worlds of unknown beauty, a naturalistic wonder, each an ecology onto itself, shunned by the local tribes for centuries. The House of the Gods was not made for men.

But now, the crew and passengers of a small charter plane are about to find what was hidden for sixty million years.

Lost on an island in the clouds 10.000 feet above the jungle, surrounded by dinosaurs, hunted by mysterious mercenaries, the survivors of Sligo Air flight 001 will quickly learn the only rule of life on Earth: Extinction.

Check out other great

Dinosaur Thrillers!

Steve Metcalf

OBJEKT 221

Ruthless multi-national conglomerate Allied Genetics is under siege from a paramilitary force for hire. Allied calls in reinforcements and fortifies their crown-jewel property – an abandoned Soviet military facility in Crimea known during the Cold War as Objekt 221. Fortunately for the future of their research, O221 straddles a stretch of rocky landscape that hides a rift – a portal through time and space. Through this rift, Allied Genetics can travel, at will, to the Cretaceous – 100 million years into Earth's past – and bolster their genetic experiments with dinosaur DNA ... something their competitors want to stop at all costs."Objekt 221" is a story blending numerous science fiction elements such as repurposed military facilities, time travel, rogue corporate armies, dinosaurs and the hint of a super-ancient civilization.

Bestselling collection

PREHISTORIC: A DINOSAUR ANTHOLOGY

PREHISTORIC is an action packed collection of stories featuring terrifying creatures that once ruled the Earth. Lost worlds where T-Rex and Velociraptors still roam and man is now on the menu. Laboratories at the forefront of cloning technology experiment with dinosaurs they do not understand or are able to contain. The deepest parts of the ocean where Megalodon, the largest and most ferocious predator to have ever existed is stalking new prey. Plus many more thrillers filled with extinct prehistoric monsters written by some of the best creature feature authors this side of the Jurassic period.

CHECK OUT OTHER GREAT DINOSAUR BOOKS

PRIMORDIA
by Greig Beck

Ben Cartwright, former soldier, home to mourn the loss of his father stumbles upon cryptic letters from the past between the author, Arthur Conan Doyle and his great, great grandfather who vanished while exploring the Amazon jungle in 1908.

Amazingly, these letters lead Ben to believe that his ancestor's expedition was the basis for Doyle's fantastical tale of a lost world inhabited by long extinct creatures. As Ben digs some more he finds clues to the whereabouts of a lost notebook that might contain a map to a place that is home to creatures that would rewrite everything known about history, biology and evolution.

But other parties now know about the notebook, and will do anything to obtain it. For Ben and his friends, it becomes a race against time and against ruthless rivals.

In the remotest corners of Venezuela, along winding river trails known only to lost tribes, and through near impenetrable jungle, Ben and his novice team find a forbidden place more terrifying and dangerous than anything they could ever have imagined.

PANGAEA EXILES
by Jeff Brackett

Tried and convicted for his crimes, Sean Barrow is sent into temporal exile—banished to a time so far before recorded history that there is no chance that he, or any other criminal sent back, has any chance of altering history.

Now Sean must find a way to survive more than 200 million years in the past, in a world populated by monstrous creatures that would rend him limb from limb if they got the chance. And that's just his fellow prisoners.

The dinosaurs are almost as bad.

www.ingramcontent.com/pod-product-compliance
Lightning Source LLC
Chambersburg PA
CBHW061239170626
46809CB00007B/2749

* 9 7 8 1 9 2 3 1 6 5 5 7 1 *